The Silent Rift

By

C. L. Roberts

Table of Contents

Part: 1

Chapter: One

I buried my wife and daughter today. They'd been dead for months, but their bodies were only found yesterday. I still can't believe they're gone.

Pacing through the condo, everything still looks untouched—just like it was the last time I left for an assignment.

I enter the living room and expect to see my two brunette women sitting on the couch, watching some love story on one of those channels. I don't recall which one—they never forced me to sit down and watch with them.

Now I wish they had. I'd give anything to have them back. Anything.

Was that my comms device chiming? Why hadn't M5 alerted me to the call?

"M5," I called out, stomping down the hallway toward the bedroom. "M5?" I repeated. Standing in the doorframe, I saw the little spherical droid lying on the unmade bed, powered off. I didn't remember doing it.

God, my memory used to be so sharp. Maybe it's the trauma of the last few days. Or maybe it's the anxiety meds the docs put me on. Whatever the case, I need to find a way through this grief and get my head cleared.

The comms device on the bed chimed again. For some reason, I hesitated to answer. It was probably someone from my team, or a high-ranking commander calling to pass on their condolences. Whoever it was, I didn't care.

So, I let it chime. Five minutes. Then ten.

In a burst of anger, I flung it out the open window and into the ruined cityscape.

I didn't watch it fall. From this height, it probably smashed on impact. Instead, I stared out at what had once been a magnificent city.

New York was mostly burnt-out buildings and craters now. Not the sparkling city of lights it used to be.

Dragging myself back to the living room, I stepped onto the balcony for a better view. If only they had stayed in the condo…they'd still be alive.

I can't let my emotions rule me. I need control. It wasn't like there was anything I could've done. If I had been with them, I would've gone into the shelter too—and died alongside them.

Isn't that what I want? To be dead with them?

I returned to the couch. First, I sat. Then I laid down. Sleep. That's what I needed. I always felt better after some rest.

I didn't even bother removing my boots. Just closing my eyes was enough to send me into a deep slumber.

Until some jackass started pounding on my door.

It was dark outside. No lights anywhere. The Artran fleet's bombing runs had knocked out most of Earth's energy grid. Thank God the war is over—at least for now.

More pounding. Incessant.

Whoever this was, they'd better have a damn good reason for waking me. Hell, it had better be the Chief and Commander of the Colonial Earth Forces himself.

Jerking open the door, I found two CEF Marines—and Admiral Thadd. The man hadn't even come to the funeral. But here he was, standing on my doorstep.

There was grief in the admiral's expression, in the way he stood with arms folded in front of him, shoulders slumped. Thadd never looked like that. He always carried himself with authority—chin up, shoulders back. Practiced posturing. It gave the illusion of power, control…everything a man in his position needed.

I had to bite my tongue before greeting him. The first words that came to mind were a string of curses.

"Jack," Thadd said. "I'm sorry about your loss. I wish I could've been at the funeral today, but with the end of the war, everything is in chaos. And you know there's nothing I wouldn't do for you."

He was buttering me up. He always got overly congenial right before dropping a major assignment. And that explained the two Marines. There were metal cuffs and tasers in their jacket pockets—that much was clear from the abnormal bulge in their right sides.

So, whatever this assignment was, I wouldn't be able to say no.

"May I come in, Jack?" Thadd asked, extending a hand.

"No," I replied. "I want to be left alone."

He lowered his hand and glanced at the Marines. "Leave me," I heard him say.

Then he looked back at me. His eyelids were drooping. His voice held hesitation. I could tell he didn't want to be here either.

"Jack…let's go inside. I hope you have some glasses—I brought a really good bourbon," he said, patting his jacket.

I couldn't confirm if he had the bottle, but he kept eye contact. That usually meant he was telling the truth.

And bourbon was one thing I wouldn't turn down.

I let him in. The condo was still pitch-black, so I cracked a few chemical glow sticks and placed them around the room and kitchen.

After rummaging around, I found two glasses and brought them back to the living room. Thadd poured a healthy amount into mine.

"To a long-lasting peace," he toasted.

"I hope you're right, Admiral," I said, taking a sip. It was good bourbon. Smooth and gentle, just like a good bottle should be.

Thadd turned and walked toward the balcony. "Jack, you know I wouldn't be here unless I had no other choice."

I stepped up beside him. The cityscape was bathed in crescent moonlight. My daughter used to call it the "fingernail moon."

Was I crying?

"Jack," he said, voice low. "I begged and pleaded with command not to give you this assignment. It's unfair and even—"

"I get it, Admiral. Just tell me what it's about."

In truth, I didn't want to know. But that wasn't going to change anything. One way or another, I was going on this mission.

"Did you hear about the incident on Septis Four?" Thadd asked.

"The attack on Novick City? I thought the military had it under control."

Thadd shook his head. "That's the official story. The truth is, once those walls were breached by the local wildlife, it's been chaos. The prisoners are free. They've taken over the city. The remaining military forces are holed up in the command tower."

"I'm a little confused, Admiral. This sounds like a job for the Marines—not a recon and infiltration squad."

"There's more. During the chaos, a couple of high-level executives visiting the Greystone Mining operation were taken hostage. So far, the more organized prisoners haven't tried to use them as leverage yet. Greystone gave us one option: get their people out alive and unharmed."

"What about the other teams?" I asked. "You could've reassigned someone."

"I tried, Jack. I really did. But with the war just ending, all our teams are on assignment. Yours is the only one I can get to Septis Four in time."

"My team can do it, Admiral. But I want it on record—I'm not mentally fit for this mission."

"Noted," Thadd replied. "Why don't you let Beverly lead the mission? You can take a backseat and help coordinate."

"I may do that, Admiral. I'll decide once we assess the situation. When do we leave?"

"Within the hour, Captain. Your team is already waiting. And once again, Jack… I'm truly sorry for your loss. And keep the bottle, it'll help."

I watched him leave through the front door, then sat down and finished the last sips of bourbon—wondering if this was the last assignment I'd ever be given. Novick city was filled with the worst of criminals. Everything from deserters to murders and serial rapist all being used as free labor for the Greystone mining operations.

This assignment wasn't going to be easy, even in Ghost armor. Instead of letting the details rule my conscious thoughts. I poured and drank more of the bourbon until I felt a little lightheaded. Before heading for the bedroom to recover M5. The team was going to need its tactical coordination and advice on this mission.

Chapter: Two

By the time I arrived at the *Elminster*, currently berthed at the New Jersey spaceport, I was greeted by a hug from Jericho. Her short brown hair smelled faintly of refried beans and a rather spicy enchilada sauce. There was also the unmistakable scent of propane lingering on her.

"And before you ask, Captain," she said, "I *did* bring the food onboard. I figured one hot meal on the journey would be better than the rations we're constantly stuck with. Also, it beats Bev's culinary tastes."

"At least I can taste my food," Beverly replied in her crisp British accent, now standing at the station immediately to my left. Her dark hair had grown out and needed trimming to meet regulation. Dark rings under her eyes and a hint of bloodshot red told me she hadn't slept well. "You put so much hot sauce in your food I can't even feel my tongue when I eat."

Jericho let go of me and moved to her pilot's seat at the front of the bridge. Bev approached me cautiously, her dark eyes scanning my face before she spoke.

"Sorry, Captain. I told Thadd that Jericho and I could handle this ourselves. Especially just hours after the funeral. It's not right."

"I know," I said. "I need you both to listen carefully."

I waited for Jericho to turn in her seat and face me.

"I've already informed Admiral Thadd that I'm mentally unfit for this assignment. It's been officially noted. What I need from both of you is your absolute best. If you see me making mistakes—or think I'm compromised—I need you to call me on it. Understood?"

"Aye, sir," they both replied in unison.

"Now let's get this tub moving. M5 will brief us on the mission along the way."

***

I don't remember when I last ate, but the enchiladas and beans were a special treat—Jericho really outdid herself. Even Beverly didn't complain, though the food was much milder than Jericho's usual fiery fare.

"Okay, M5, show us the details."

M5 was plugged into his station directly behind my co-pilot's chair. Jericho sat to my left, Beverly at the intelligence station behind her.

"Bringing it up on the hologram display," M5 said through our neural link.

The large parasteel window at the front of the ship projected a holographic image: a detailed scene showing the bodies of many large, four-legged creatures strewn at the breached perimeter of the multi-layered, pyramid-shaped building that housed Novick City.

The top of the pyramid had been flattened and converted into the main military operations base. Even though the Greystone Mining Corporation owned and built the complex, the Colonial Earth Forces was deeply embedded—after all, Greystone was the top ore manufacturer for both shipbuilding and personal armor.

"So, what happened here?" Bev asked.

"According to the classified files we were given," M5 explained, "a lone alien Nomad survivor from Chevron Five lured the beasts near the city to incite an attack. The Bomar beasts are sensitive to certain sounds and vibrations and they have attacked the city many times before in the past. Despite the efforts of both the Corporation and the CEF to keep them away, the Nomad's motivation was to use the chaos as cover to kidnap a prisoner and extract information from him."

"Did he think the prisoner knew something about the atmosphere generator destruction on his world?" Jericho asked.

"That remains unknown, as does the Nomad's current whereabouts," M5 replied.

"That's fine, M5," I said. "The Nomad is irrelevant to our mission. But tell me—is this holographic feed live?"

"It is, Captain. The prisoners appear to be cutting up the Bomar bodies—likely for food or fuel. The remaining military presence has shut off all incoming supplies."

"How long has that been going on?" Bev asked.

"Fifty-three hours. Fighting is ongoing within the city, and there is a small organized effort underway to seize control of the central command. All prisoner tracking devices are still functional, as are those of the executives. They're currently located in Prison Facility Beta."

"Great," Jericho muttered. "A snatch-and-grab op—with thousands of inmates running wild."

"Look at it this way," I said. "At least they're not completely organized. That gives us room to maneuver—if we're smart."

"Have there been any demands regarding the executives?" Beverly asked, arms folded across her chest.

"None," I said.

"Surely the prisoners know who they are—and their value," Jericho said.

She was right. It made no sense. Why hadn't the prisoners used them for leverage?

"Whatever the reason, our job is to go in, extract the executives, and clear the way for the Marines to come in and mop up."

"I will be sending each of you a packet," M5 said. "It includes an updated map of the facility and facial recognition data, uploaded to your armor HUDs."

"Let's do this job quick and clean, ladies. Pack a few extra ammo cartridges, just in case. We'll be landing on top of Novick City in three hours. Get ready."

I watched as Jericho and Beverly exited the bridge through the rear portal hatch. I should've followed them—but something made me linger.

My eyes drifted to the hologram of the city. My heart rate ticked upward. Then, without warning, an image flashed in my mind: a body lying in the sand… someone kneeling beside it. The vision was distant, blurry. I couldn't make out any details. Then it vanished.

"Captain," M5 said, "the odds of mission success for you and your team are well over seventy-five percent. I recommend that you relax—perhaps perform your Wing Chun kata before suiting up. That always helps settle your thoughts."

"I might do that," I said, turning to leave the bridge.

But the image lingered.

Negative thoughts before a mission weren't unusual—I often treated them as hypothetical "what if" scenarios. But this…this felt colder. Sharper.

A chill ran up my spine.

It had to be the meds. Just a side effect.

I'd be glad once they were out of my system.

Because I'm not psychic.

And I don't believe in that kind of thing.

Chapter: Three

A dust storm had blown in over the city, making visibility impossible to the naked eye. M5 was piloting the ship, and in a small visual display to my upper right, I could see the holographic trajectory he was following all the way to the rooftop.

There was a brief *thump* as the vessel touched down. The back ramp descended slowly. Jericho led the way. Through my helmet visor, I could see her in the familiar matte-black armor of the Ghost Recon suits. The HUD was providing the simulated image, based on our locations. Because if I were looking with the naked eye—or even with thermal or infrared—I wouldn't see her. The suits were designed to phase the wearer partially out of all visible spectrums. Even sound was muted by the cloaking field. In reality, they were more nonexistent than ghosts.

"The maintenance elevator is up ahead," M5 said through my helmet speaker.

The dust cloud was thick, and without the holographic recreation of the environment around us, we would have been blind. The storm worked in our favor. With the wall breached, the storm was flooding into the interior, affecting the prisoners' visibility as well.

"Do you have the door for us, M5?" Jericho asked. "Or will I have to bypass it?"

"The power has been cut," M5 replied. "New update: the executives are still in the Beta prison complex—third floor, cell 337."

"Good to know, M5," I said. "Jericho, how's the door coming?"

"Just like stealing cars back home, Captain."

It took both Beverly and Jericho to muscle the door open. Once it was done, I peered down the metal shaft into the city. The dust cloud had billowed in, masking much of the interior, but as we rappelled down, I spotted glow sticks and flashlights dancing below. Some areas were even well-lit, likely using backup power. It supported M5's theory that the Bomar remains were being used as a fuel source.

I was the first to land on top of the elevator cage at the bottom. According to the thermal overlay on my helmet display, two bodies were inside.

The hatch opened easily.

One of the men inside looked up—just in time for me to slam down, stabbing my blade into his jugular. The other didn't get a chance to react. I put a bullet through his head before he could make a sound.

Unfortunate. But they were obstacles. The safety of my team and the mission came first.

Jericho followed, then Beverly.

"Take the lead," I told Beverly, standing just outside the elevator, scanning the surroundings.

M5 projected an overhead map of the city on the right-hand portion of my visor, highlighting nearby inmate tracking IDs and drawing a red path toward our objective.

"Looks good, M5," Bev said, motioning for us to move forward.

She set a good pace. After bypassing several sentries stationed outside the prison, we entered the complex. All the gates had been unlocked and left open. There might have been three or four prisoners assigned to guard the high-value targets, but the ones we encountered just seemed to be wandering aimlessly.

Not at all what I expected to encounter.

"Captain," Bev said, "something isn't right."

Jericho joined in. "Agreed. This is becoming annoyingly too easy. I think my five-year-old nephew could've staged something better than these inmates."

"M5, what's the status of the fighting at the command tower?" Bev asked over the open comms.

It was a good question. Perhaps the prisoners with a vested interest in the executives had committed most of their forces to taking the tower. After all, it was the key to the whole city.

"Based on my analysis of the ongoing conflict and communications with the Colonial Earth Forces," M5 responded, "they are losing ground to the prisoners."

"Looking at the tracker IDs," I said, "it looks like the prisoners outnumber the CEF two to one."

M5 replied, "Many of the CEF officers were killed during the chaos of the Bomar attacks. At the rate the prisoners are gaining territory, I estimate the tower will be taken over in the next couple of hours."

"No pressure," Jericho muttered.

"That gives us plenty of time to get the executives and escape. Then the Marines can do their thing."

"Amen," Jericho said.

"Enough chatter," I ordered. "Let's get this mission over with quickly. I don't want to deal with the organized prisoners."

We ascended three flights of stairs. My heart was racing—more from a nagging sense of unease than from exertion. At the entrance to

Cell 337, Beverly and Jericho came to a stop. According to the executive tracker IDs, this was the right location.

But what we found inside wasn't them.

Two males in prison uniforms lay atop one another, throats slit. Above their bodies, scrawled in blood, was a single word:

TRAITORS

Why kill them? They might be traitors, but they were the best bargaining chip they had. It didn't make sense.

"Now what, Captain?" Jericho asked.

Chapter: Four

It's my belief that no crime scene is ever left completely clean. There's always some devil hiding in the details. I just had to coax it out of hiding.

"Jericho, keep watch," I said, bending down to examine the bodies more closely. "Beverly, do a quick sweep of this floor. See if we missed anything along the way."

"On it," Bev replied.

I lifted one of the dead men's heads into my hands, bringing it closer to my visual sensors while M5 fed me data through our neural link.

"Captain, these men are not the executives. According to my facial recognition, this is Inmate 1127, James Husk, and Inmate 0827, Patrick Combs," M5 said.

Why would someone go to the effort of misdirecting us?

"Bev, Jericho," I said over the open comms, "these are not our executives. Stay frosty."

M5 continued reporting his findings: "The cut to the throat was shallow, severing the vocal cords and barely nicking the carotid artery. Hence the lack of blood spray patterns. This man bled out slowly—intentionally."

"Why were they labeled as traitors?" I asked out loud.

"It's possible, Captain, that they were informing on others," M5 replied. "However, there's no indication of cooperation in their criminal records."

Turning the head slightly, my thumb found a wound at the base of the skull. I examined the round puncture more closely.

"Is it a bullet wound?" I asked.

"Negative, Captain,"M5 answered. "It was created by a sharp, narrow object. Reason unknown. Likely postmortem."

I moved to the next body—a younger man—and began examining the knife wound to his throat.

"The cut is nearly identical," M5 noted. "At this point, I would hypothesize the killer had some surgical training."

"My thoughts exactly," I said, now checking the back of his neck for a matching puncture. I found it.

Then I discovered the small metallic tracking devices in their pockets—and something else. A scalpel. Despite the blood smear, a thumbprint was still visible.

M5 ran it through the database.

"Match found. Doctor Evan Kimbel. Age twenty-five. Recently graduated medical school. Assigned to the community clinic near the maintenance elevator shaft."

What could've driven someone like that to do this?

"Captain," Beverly said over comms. "You need to see this."

"On our way," I said, tapping Jericho on the shoulder. "M5, show me the current location of Doctor Evan Kimbel."

My helmet display zoomed in on the clinic.

"He's been there for the past five hours," M5 confirmed.

I was about to thank him when my voice caught. On the second floor of the prison, Beverly stood outside a cell with three more bodies inside—throats slashed, the word **TRAITORS** written above them in blood. Almost an exact replica of the first scene.

"There are at least two more cells on this floor with bodies just like this," Beverly said. "I can't make sense of it, Captain. It's like a madman did this."

"Then let's go talk to the madman. M5 shows he's still at the clinic."

"Want me to take point?" Beverly asked.

"No. I've got it. Let's move out."

***

Despite the worsening dust storm as we neared the clinic, M5 displayed a large concentration of convicts gathering near a brightly lit structure labeled *The Xanadu*—a nightclub and brothel. The smell of roasting Bomar meat drifted from nearby fire pits.

"Looks like a party, Captain," Jericho muttered.

"Let's hope they stay entertained," I replied as we reached the dark clinic's front door. Power was out, and no other tracking IDs were inside—except for the doctor's.

"Captain," M5 warned. "I've detected a sudden radioactive spike in your area."

"Any idea what it was?" I asked, sweeping my weapon ahead and turning right at the T-intersection.

"After analysis, your suits have been exposed to a radioactive isotope. It won't make you visible, but anyone with a radiation detector can track your general direction within a short range."

"Great. We've walked into a trap," I muttered. "Jericho, take the far door. Bev, go back to the T-section and monitor for activity. M5, bring them up to speed. I'm pressing forward."

Their voices bantered in my headset, but my attention was locked on the room ahead. It was a morgue—refrigerated cubbies for corpses and a central steel medical table.

The signal led me to one of the middle drawers. I opened it slowly, pistol ready.

No surprise: the body of Evan Kimbel lay inside. Still clothed. Eyes open.

I examined the corpse—no bullet wounds, no punctures. But his eyes were bloodshot, his nostril stained with fresh blood, and three faint circular burns marked his forehead.

"Captain, without a blood sample, I can't determine the cause of death," M5 said.

"It's okay, M5. I think I just found what the killer *wanted* us to find."

I picked up the left hand and spotted a faint blue glow under the fingernail.

"I know what this is," I muttered. "Phosphorescent cave mold."

"Only found in the sealed mine shafts in Alpha Block," M5 replied. "Some of those shafts were flooded."

"Someone's playing with us. Leaving breadcrumbs."

"There are several military prisoners here, Captain," M5 said. "None have Ghost Recon clearance or relatives with connections to the program."

"Captain," Jericho interrupted. "We're about to have company. At least a dozen prisoners, armed, moving this way."

"Bev, Jericho—stand by for orders."

Whoever was behind this knew our suit's vulnerability. The isotope compromised our stealth. Sure, we could vanish from light and sound—but not bullets.

Still, the isotope worked both ways.

"M5, display military prisoner records on the left-hand HUD," I said, leaving the morgue and heading down the corridor. Water wasn't running—no chance to wash the isotope off—but there had to be alternatives.

The maintenance closet was just ahead, already partially ajar. A body lay inside—older man, long gray hair, blood matted into his scalp. On the back of his gray jumpsuit, the word **TRAITOR** was smeared in blood.

I knelt to inspect him.

There it was again: the same skull puncture wound.

"Captain," Jericho's voice crackled. "They're breaching the west side door. Won't take them long to find the main entrance."

"Understood," I replied. "Bev, Jericho—plant trip explosives at both hallway entrances. Fall back to the morgue. I'll meet you shortly."

They acknowledged, but I was already elbow-deep in the closet, digging through supplies.

Then I found it: a canister of powdered chemical spill solvent. Bentonite clay.

It could bond with the isotope and allow us to brush it off. A crude but effective solution. The question was: How could I use this to our advantage?

Canister in hand, I headed back toward the morgue, scrolling through M5's prisoner list. Then I froze mid-stride.

One name at the bottom:

Walter Sickert
Birthplace: Munich, Germany
Date of Birth: May 30

"What the hell…" I whispered, resuming my pace just as a flash of light from an explosion lit up the corridor ahead.

Was someone mocking me? Testing me? Or had I finally stepped into something I couldn't control?

That name…that birthdate…matched one of the suspects in the *Jack the Ripper* case. I knew this because of our criminal mind classes at the academy. It had to be a falsified entry—but why plant such an obvious clue?

"Walter is currently located in the Xanadu club," M5 reported. "Only Commander Grant had authority to modify prisoner files, although doing so violates multiple CEF regulations."

"Do you have an image of this prisoner?"

"No, Captain."

Was this the person behind the killings? Or just another breadcrumb? It felt like someone was spoon-feeding me a narrative—guiding me to a conclusion.

And then—

The shooting began.

Chapter: Five

Narrowly dodging a couple of stray shots that shattered the concrete walls of the hallway, I made it back to the morgue. Beverly and Jericho stood on either side of the doorway, firing their rifles down the corridor.

There was no sound from them, but through my mind's eye I could see a prisoner fall with every one of their trigger pulls. I didn't waste time talking. Instead, I scooped the powder onto Beverly's suit, then we switched places, and she did the same for me.

While I stood in the doorway, two prisoners tossed a flashbang in an attempt to disorient us. What they didn't know was that our suit's helmet shielded us from such tactics. Two clean shots—two more prisoners down, both taken out with headshots.

A tap on the shoulder signaled that Beverly was done, and we switched places again.

"What's the play here, Captain?" Beverly asked.

"Jericho, I want you to keep these prisoners busy. Lead them to the south end of the city. Be prepared to evacuate through the crack in the wall."

"I get to play bait," Jericho said. "I like it, Captain. I'll try not to kill them all."

"What's my role?" Beverly asked.

"I need you to check the mining tunnels in Alpha Block. I believe our executives are being held captive there—but watch yourself. Whoever's behind this is clever and competent. They know how our teams operate."

"Then I'll be more clever," Beverly said. "And what about you?"

"I'm going after the puppeteer."

I stepped away from them, walked to the rear wall of the morgue, and placed a sticky explosive charge.

"Take cover," I ordered, giving it twenty seconds before pressing the red button on my wrist console.

The gray wall blew outward, leaving a hole large enough for us to pass through one at a time. Once outside, we split off, each heading toward our objectives.

"The command center has fallen," M5 reported. "Commander Grant and her staff have been taken hostage."

"Thanks for the update. Got any tactical intel for me?"

"One item: the prisoners who attacked you at the clinic were all wearing red bandanas on their left arms—unlike the others. My analysis indicates that this is the organized group."

"And the traitor killings?"

"Despite extensive research through historical records, I've found no precedent. And without Commander Grant's codes, I can't access the local administration systems."

"Then we figure this out on our own. Bring up the overlay of the brothel—and my target."

"Walter has not moved," M5 confirmed. "However, several non-inmates have interacted with him."

Prostitutes, most likely.

As I approached the crowd surrounding the building, it felt like a tailgate party—bottled beers, fire pits cooking Bomar meat, casual chatter, even makeshift games of cornhole.

None of the local prisoners wore red bandanas. A few were armed with pistols or improvised weapons. Despite the relaxed atmosphere, many kept glancing toward the central building at the city's center.

Faint gunfire echoed from that direction. Not all of the CEF had surrendered yet. I wished I could help them, but my mission was clear. The best thing I could do—for them—was get the executives out and get the hell off this rock. Then the Marines could clean up the rest.

The club's front entrance was too crowded, so I opted for the side service door. It was open. A few men in stained white T-shirts were hauling out garbage bags to a nearby waste bin. I slipped in behind them, moving through the busy kitchen.

I bumped into a few people, but no one noticed. With this many bodies, jostling was expected.

The kitchen exited near a carpeted stairwell. My target was on the third floor. As I neared the hallway entrance, I paused on a lower step to let two bandana-wearing prisoners pass by.

Two more followed behind.

"I found the executives," Beverly's voice came over the comms. "And Captain—you're not going to like the ugly technology I just discovered."

I stepped back onto the central platform, pressed myself against the wall, and watched the stairwell. I had a good vantage point—enough to stay hidden for a minute or two.

"Explain, Beverly."

"A section of the mines has been turned into a makeshift prison—and possibly a medical facility. But the equipment looks more like torture devices. I've never seen anything like it."

"M5?"

"This equipment matches nothing in my database. It may be alien or proprietary to Greystone Mining Corporation."

"Something else," Beverly added. "Those three spherical marks on the doctor's forehead—you remember them? I think this equipment caused them."

Could the CEF really be allowing prisoners to be experimented on? And for what purpose? Illegal. Unethical.

I took a deep breath and exhaled slowly.

"Document everything. M5, bring the *Elminster* down to the ground, outside the breach in the wall—just past the Bomar bodies. Bev, I'll meet you and Jericho there soon."

"Understood, sir. And Captain…good luck."

I didn't usually rely on luck.

But the moment I stepped into the third-floor hallway, everything changed.

Half a dozen red-bandana-wearing prisoners turned toward me in perfect unison.

Another trap.

Never in my life had I been played like this—but it was game time now.

And I raised my rifle.

Chapter: Six

The hallway was narrow, dim, and reeked of cigarettes and alcohol. I took advantage of the prisoners who had spread out from the pack gathered outside the target's door. A precise shot to one prisoner's chest nearby left him stunned and dumbfounded.

Smashing my helmet into his face I hoisted the barely conscious person onto my shoulder, and used his body as a shield to push deeper down the hallway. The man didn't stand a chance—as his fellow prisoners opened fire, their rounds tore into his back, hoping to hit me behind him. Only the attackers wielding AKs posed a real threat to my armor.

The small-caliber pistols were a joke, even at point-blank range. Knives, on the other hand, could find their way into the jointed areas. I was still invisible to them. If I had to guess, someone had installed old-school pressure plates in the hallway—low-tech and easy to overlook. It had to have sent an alert to them in some fashion. I would have to review the combat footage later to find what I had missed. Right now, I felt like a fool. I should have noticed the bandana-wearing prisoners avoiding specific sections of the floor.

A couple of shots struck me from behind, nearly knocking me off balance. Two shotgun-wielding inmates had entered the fray, placing me in the middle of a kill box.

To hell with them.

Using the corpse in my arms, I rushed into the trio still huddled near the door. I struck the AK-wielding prisoner first, smashing the butt of my rifle into his face. He reeled back, dazed, no longer a threat. I spun around behind him, firing wildly at the other two.

Fortunately, they were so close together it was impossible to miss—and none of them wore body armor. My rounds shredded them where they stood.

Down the corridor, the shotgun carriers opened fire again. This time, the broken-nose prisoner caught the blasts square in the chest—buying me the time I needed to line up two clean shots. One to the first shotgun-wielder's head, and an instant follow-up to the second.

Six bodies now littered the hallway. I'd taken a few hits, but the armor was holding.

Fueled by adrenaline, I kicked in the target's door and found the room empty—except for a fire spreading quickly across the curtains and walls. A toppled oil lamp looked to be the culprit. The windows were barred. The only exit was a secondary door, which led to another bedroom.

A couple in the next room. One male that the HUD quickly identified as prisoner 2129. Kevin G. Parsons was engaged in a sexual act with Greystone employee 77169, Jenifer Grey. They scrambled to throw on clothes, panic etched across their faces as the fire spread into their space. Walter had clearly come through here— and continued through another set of doors. Beyond that, there shouldn't have been anywhere else to go… unless—

I stepped into the adjoining room and froze.

A stripper pole ran through the center of the room, dropping two floors down to the club's main level.

Several mostly naked women stood frozen in fear. A few were peering down through the opening. My HUD tracker lit up—my target was now on the main floor, sprinting for the exit.

At this rate, he could escape—or worse, lead me straight into another ambush.

I needed a different approach.

Smashing through the working girls' bedroom door sent them into screaming panic—an unseen force ripping through their space. I crossed the hallway and burst into another room. Despite the barred window, the rest of the material beyond it was made of glass. Through the scope, I spotted my target by having the HUD display zoom in on his tracking ID —a dark figure sprinting across the open plaza.

The first bullet clipped him in the shoulder. He tumbled to the ground.

I watched him try to rise, staggering forward.

The second shot struck him in the thigh—dead center. He collapsed, screaming.

I jogged out of the club toward him. The surrounding prisoners had already fled. No one came to his aid. I approached cautiously.

Then M5's voice exploded into my neural link—sharp and chaotic:

"Ship systems being overridden…"

Then silence.

No matter how many times I tried to reach the ship—or my team—I was met with nothing.

The realization crept through me like an arctic wind—up my legs, through my arms, and out the top of my skull.

I flipped the target onto his back, staring into his face. Examining his arms, I found a long, narrow scar across the wrist— exactly where a tracker would be implanted.

This man's tracker had been removed.

Lifting him closer to my helmet, I powered off the phase cloak. Now he could see me. Hear me.

"Where is the person that this tracker belongs to?"

His eyes were wild, tear-streaked.

"Don't kill me! Don't kill me! I'll serve the Artrans—I swear it!"

What the hell was he talking about?

Didn't he know the war with the Artrans was over?

"Where is the man you're impersonating? What's his name?"

"Ethan," the man bellowed. "He told me if I wanted to protect my family, my friends—we had to eliminate the Artran traitors. I *saw* one of them, man! Controlling someone's body—telepathic or something!"

"Ethan's last name?"

"Lineberry, I think."

I released him.

His upper torso flopped back to the ground with a dull thud.

That name.

It wasn't possible.

Ethan Lineberry was dead. His entire team—dead. I was there the day they buried him. I held his wife's hand. I consoled his children.

It just wasn't possible.

Chapter: Seven

The idea of Artran telepaths was completely absurd.

Before I became a Ghost Recon operative, I had been an intelligence officer. One of my first assignments had been to analyze the enemy for any signs of special abilities—telepathy, psychokinesis, anything unusual. Some of the stories my team had collected from the lizard-like aliens known as the Nomads spoke of the Artran's past—of a great galactic war they had fought against a powerful telepathic race referred to only as the Ancients. It was said the war began because the Ancients could not control or pacify the Artrans.

And it was true: every Artran prisoner they tested had failed—telepathically immune.

If the person pulling the strings was a former Ghost operative—or had insider knowledge—that could explain how they were staying one step ahead of me.

But what about M5's cryptic message?

Ship systems being overridden.

How could that be done? A computer virus introduced from inside the ship, maybe?

No. No. No.

Reactivating the cloaking field, I sprinted toward the breach in the city wall. Incoherent thoughts raced through my mind.

Was my team still alive? Was the ship still there?

Just as I passed through one of the large, damaged sections, the sandstorm had slowed enough for me to see the *Elminster* lifting into the sky.

Nearby, I saw two figures—one lying on their back, the other kneeling over them. It was the same scene I'd seen in the cockpit several hours ago. My body froze as the implications hit me.

Had that alien technology done something to me? It had been a few years ago since I had stood before the alien thing me and Ethan had nicknamed the Omega Mirror.

I ran, heart pounding, until I reached them.

Jericho was on the ground—eyes closed, helmet off, upper armor removed. Beverly had wrapped some bandages around her chest, but blood was still seeping through.

Decloaking, I was now phased back in to all visible light, and I knelt beside her.

"She's losing a lot of blood," Beverly said. "I need to get her to the medical facility."

Getting to my feet, I helped lift Jericho onto Beverly's shoulder.

"What happened?" I asked.

"The executives turned on us," Beverly said. "Before I knew what was happening, one of them shot Jericho with her own pistol. The other inserted a device into an open terminal. Then everything went dark—power fluctuated, screens went blank, and M5 stopped functioning."

"We've been played since the moment we arrived," I said. "The target I was chasing wasn't even the right one. He believed Artran telepaths were controlling people."

"That's what I heard the executives muttering just before a third person arrived—pulling a black-cart with several nuclear warhead cores. I couldn't see his face because of the mask he wore, but...something about him felt familiar."

"Did he say anything to you?"

"No. The executives ordered me off the ship with Jericho."

"Get her to the med center," I ordered, turning back toward the city.

"Jack, what the hell is going on?" Beverly called after me.

"Not completely sure. But I have to stop that ship before it reaches its target."

The only way to do that was to reach the top level of the command center and access the communications array. Even if the ship's systems were compromised, the insurgence device was tied to the fusion reactor—independent of the core systems. It had been installed months ago as a failsafe. If CEF technology ever fell into Artran or other alien hands, it could be remotely destroyed.

The catch? I needed Commander Grant's access codes.

Finding her without M5's tactical support from the ship wasn't going to be easy. I'd have to do this the old-fashioned way.

***

As I neared the central tower, the interior of Novick City was lit by uncontrolled fire. The *Xanadu* brothel was fully engulfed, and nearby buildings were catching as well. Without access to the city's water supply, the fire would keep spreading.

The death toll would be catastrophic—prisoners dying not just from fire, but from toxic smoke inhalation. Without the main air circulation fans, the entire city would choke.

This gave me another reason to reach the command center—activate the fans, start fire suppression, and save whoever I could.

The thick double doors of the central tower were halfway open when I arrived. To my surprise, there were no guards posted. I walked right in.

The lower level was a garage for riot-control vehicles and fuel reserves. Emergency lights gave just enough illumination to move without night vision.

I ascended the stairwell. Around the tenth level, my enhanced audio package picked up two men talking. From the schematics I'd memorized, I knew the tenth floor housed administrators and CEF officers.

Could Grant be held in her own quarters?

I paused, listening. Only two voices. The others had likely been sent to handle the fire.

Decloaking by phasing in, I hollered up the stairwell.

"Fire in the bay! Get your asses down here to help out!"

Then I phased out and slammed the main stairwell door shut behind me.

The two guards rushed down the steps—right into my trap.

I took out the first with a rifle butt to the back of the head. He dropped instantly.

The second turned, confused, and caught a strike to the face before he could react.

Both prisoners were down and unconscious. I estimated I had several minutes before they came to.

Sprinting up the stairs two at a time, I found the tenth-floor door slightly ajar. Carpeted floors, off-white painted walls, and decorative artwork gave the space a *resort-like vibe*—a stark contrast to the chaos below.

One prisoner stood guard at a nearby door, shotgun in one hand, cigar in the other.

My audio picked up voices behind him, through the door.

"How many more officers do we have to execute before you give us the code?" a thin, mousy voice demanded.

I didn't need confirmation. Grant was inside. She was the only one with the lockout codes.

Striding up, I snatched the shotgun from the guard's hand and struck him in the throat. He dropped to his knees, choking.

A follow-up strike with my rifle butt dropped him flat.

I prepped the next phase.

Sticking a small explosive charge to the door, I knocked loudly, then stepped back.

Inside, I heard confusion—someone approached.

As soon as the lock clicked, I detonated the charge.

The door blew inward, knocking down the nearest person and disorienting the rest.

One prisoner scrambled for his weapon—*too slow*. I shot him in the head.

Another fumbled with a gun, shaking so badly he couldn't aim. Another clean shot.

A third wasn't as stunned—he fired a shotgun blast. My helmet blinked red: cloak offline. Armor compromised.

I was visible now. Possibly vulnerable.

Another shot came from the left. I felt the sting in my side—but adrenaline pushed me forward. I returned fire, dropping the shotgun wielder.

Diving and rolling, I came up kneeling. A wild barrage whizzed overhead. One round clipped my shoulder. Pain surged, but the armor held. I fired—another target down.

Room clear.

Commander Grant sat tied to a chair—bloody, bruised. Her long red hair matted with gore. One green eye swollen shut. The other fixed on me.

At her sides were two dead officers, shot execution-style.

Using my blade, I cut her bindings and helped her up.

"We need to reach the command center," I said. "I need access to the communications array—urgently."

She didn't speak. Just nodded.

We made our way to the main elevator and rode it up.

To my surprise, the command center was empty.

Outside the massive parasteel window, I could see why.

The city was burning.

Grant limped to the central console, fingers flying over controls.

Within seconds, I heard the hum of ventilation systems kicking in. Smoke began rising toward the ceiling. Then came the soft, rhythmic patter—rain. Fire suppression was online.

The city would survive. Some lives would be spared.

Now came the hard part.

I stepped beside her and removed my helmet.

"Tell me about Ethan Lineberry."

Her one good eye locked onto mine.

Chapter: Eight

"Ethan is not the man you knew," Grant said. "When he was brought to us—after killing his own teammates—doctors were brought in to assess his medical and mental condition."

"Ethan wouldn't have killed his team," I replied, feeling my voice rise. "I knew this man. I trained with him. I even ate dinner at his family's house."

Grant slowly shook her head.

"You don't understand. Something happened to him on his last mission. He suffered a head injury. The crew thought he was fine, but that's when he turned. He accused them of being controlled by Artran telepaths."

"Was Ethan influenced or manipulated by a telepath?" I asked.

"No," she said firmly. "The injury he sustained was to his prefrontal cortex. That's what triggered the homicidal behavior."

I slammed my palms down on the console. Leaning in closer, I stared her down.

"That can't be true. He was experimented on—just like the tests you've been running in the old mines. You did something to his mind, and it drove him insane. The CEF did this."

Grant stood, a grimace tightening her expression.

"I swear to you, everything I've told you is true. I'll even give you the medical records. Doctors spent months trying to reverse the damage to his brain. In the end, it was hopeless. He even tried using his telepathic abilities to manipulate them—to escape."

"That information is classified, Commander," I said.

"Yes, I know. I was cleared to learn about it the moment they brought him here. I thought it was insane for the CEF to assign me a homicidal telepath, but the doctors had methods of suppressing his ability."

"So, what happened, Commander? From everything I saw out there, it looks like Ethan's had his abilities for a lot longer than a couple of days."

She looked away and sighed.

"His body grew immune to the medications. Before we knew it, he had followers—people who believed the visions he implanted in their minds. They thought the Artrans were controlling everyone from behind the scenes. Deaths began to happen. And before we could implement countermeasures, everything went to hell—because of that damn Nomad named Colbosh."

"And what would your countermeasures have been, Commander?" I asked, my nails digging into my palms.

"We would've increased the dosage. Then we would have isolated him from the general population. Which, in hindsight, should've been done from the beginning."

"So, you would've locked him up in the old mines. I've seen your makeshift prison down there. I've seen the unidentified tech being used. There are laws against torturing prisoners."

"No matter what you think of me, Captain, I have superiors to answer to—just like you. I don't have the luxury of arguing over morality."

At least she was telling the truth. Too many officers looked the other way, justifying their actions in the name of ending the war.

"If you're done judging me," she said coldly, "your friend Ethan is gone. Whatever you need to do—do it."

I straightened up and stepped away from her.

I knew what I had to do.

Kill a friend.

I didn't know if I could.

I closed my eyes, took a deep breath, and calmed the storm in my head.

Then I moved to the console by the parasteel window and entered the command code. It was successful—the signal failed to send a second time, confirming that it had gone through.

Grant was already on the line with CEF command, calling for reinforcements. I sent the final transmission: confirmation that the *Elminster* was compromised and clearance for full engagement was authorized.

I don't remember what happened next. I found a chair. My heart was racing. There was a painful feeling in my gut.

And then—everything went black.

***

I saw myself in the shimmering reflection of the Omega Mirror. The longer I stared, the more convinced I became that something else was staring back—peering into me, judging me.

There was an annoying buzzing noise in my right ear followed by a sudden chill before the room around me vanished.

I was floating in space—but not as a body.

Massive alien ships battled around me. Beam weapons of green and gold tore through the void. There was no sound. Only the sensation of scale, power, and inevitability.

I didn't have time to make sense of it before the vision shifted again.

Now I was looking up at a crack in a colossal wall, a city ablaze behind me. Heat scorched my skin. I couldn't breathe. I felt myself choking.

And then a hand grabbed my shoulder and yanked me back.

"It had you deep," Ethan said, his blue eyes scanning my face. "Jack—are you okay?"

I nodded slowly, stepping away from the mirror.

"What the hell was that?" I asked.

"Alien tech," he said. "The CEF found it in one of the Ancients' cities—out on the other side of the galaxy."

"Let me guess: they want us to figure out if it's useful for the war effort."

"Thadd said you were the smart one," Ethan replied with a smirk. "So, what's your assessment?"

I rubbed my face with my hands, glancing back at the alien device. The shimmering portal had vanished, leaving a smooth, dark oval in its place.

"At first, it felt like someone was observing me. Reading my mind. Judging me."

Ethan nodded.

"And then came the visions?"

"Yes," I said, surprised we'd had similar experiences.

"Don't you love this job?" Ethan said, "The mystery of it all."

"Not when I can't even begin to fathom the reason behind it."

"Nonsense," Ethan replied. "I can tell you what it's for."

"I'm listening."

"Aside from the visions, I heard voices—like I was connected to everyone and everything at once. I'm convinced this device was made to test psionic ability. I'm certain of it."

"That's one working hypothesis," I said. "But I'm not convinced."

He just smiled and pointed to the device again.

"Ready for round two?"

I stepped forward, and the shimmering field reactivated.

This time, when I looked into my own eyes—

I saw the void staring back.

***

When I woke again, I heard the steady beeping of medical monitors. I was lying in a hospital bed, covered in a white sheet.

Beverly stood at the foot of the bed.

"Took you long enough, Captain."

I nodded. My throat felt like sandpaper. She handed me a cup of water.

"Jericho's fine—she's recovering," she said. "You, on the other hand, had to have your gallbladder removed. That bullet tore it up pretty badly."

"Where are we?" I asked.

"Funny answer… We're aboard the *Jericho*."

"Thadd's flagship?"

She nodded.

"He told me to notify him the moment you woke up. He should be here soon."

"Thank you, Beverly. You saved us both."

"Actually, you owe your life to Commander Grant. Her fast action got you stabilized long enough for surgery."

"Then I'll thank her personally."

The door opened. Admiral Thadd entered in full uniform, every bit the man on a mission.

"Thanks for the alert," he said to Beverly. "Would you give us a moment?"

She saluted, gave me a glance, and exited.

"Sorry to hit you with this so soon, Jack," Thadd said, stepping closer. "But I need to confirm a few things."

"Understood, Admiral."

I shifted upright as best I could.

"Did you send the insurgent code to the *Elminster*?"

"Yes. I had no choice."

"Did the executives go with Ethan willingly?"

"They did."

"How would you judge their mental state?"

I hesitated.

"They were under Ethan's influence. Completely."

"Do you have any idea what their target was?"

"No. But it shouldn't matter anymore." I paused, watching his face. "Unless there's something you're not telling me?"

Thadd looked toward the door, then back at me.

"This stays between us, Jack. But there's a rumor that the *Elminster's* crew was removed before you sent the code. No confirmation—just whispers."

"Understood. May I speak freely?"

"Always."

"Why didn't you tell me the truth about Ethan?"

He looked away, collected himself, then met my eyes.

"Because I knew you'd try to help him. And I couldn't let that happen. The man we knew… He was gone. What remained was a telepathic fanatic—convinced the Artrans were pulling every string in the galaxy. I recommended euthanasia. The High Council refused. They wanted to study him. Study the power he gained from the Omega Mirror."

My fists clenched the bed sheets. I forced myself to breathe, to stay calm.

He was right.

They should've ended Ethan's suffering—not turned him into a test subject.

"I know that's hard to hear," Thadd said. "But it's the truth. I've always tried to be honest with you. I did everything I could. Get some rest. A lieutenant will come later for a full report."

He left.

And I had nothing to say.

Sleep was the furthest thing from my mind.

What else was the CEF hiding from me?

If they found out I was showing signs of telepathic intuition…

Would they lock me up too?

Would I become the next Ethan?

I didn't know what path I was on anymore.

But after everything that had happened—

I wasn't sure I wanted to stay with the CEF.

Eventually, sleep found me.

And I gave in to the comfort of the blackness.

Chapter: Nine

The journey back to Earth would take a couple of days, even in jump space. I was finally allowed to get up and move around on my own—but only in short intervals.

Jericho was also up and about. Judging by the brisk power walk she was doing around the medical bay, she was clearly pushing herself to get back into action.

I worried about her sometimes. She was intelligent and bright, but she enjoyed the violence and killing a little too much. Perfect for wartime—but with the war winding down, she was going to have a hard time adjusting back to civilian life.

I'd need to talk to Admiral Thadd about her—once I was cleared for active service again. That's assuming I even decided to stay in the CEF. The idea of civilian life was becoming more appealing. At least I'd be away from the constant deception and moral compromises. My thoughts were a mess, and I needed time to sort them out.

***

Later that evening, as I lay in my medical bed flipping through news channels without really watching them, Beverly and Jericho entered the room. They were carrying an open-top box and the inner framework of a DIM-series droid.

"We brought you a gift," Beverly said. "Figured you were bored out of your mind, so we got permission from Admiral Thadd to give you the parts to reconstruct M5."

"That'll definitely help keep my hands—and my mind—active," I said as she placed the box down on the bed in front of me.

It would take weeks to rebuild a DIM-series droid. I knew that firsthand—I had been part of the original team that designed them.

"I thought you'd be power-walking with me by now, Captain," Jericho said. "I see you in the hallway every morning and afternoon."

"You're a few years younger than me, Jericho. I'm getting to be an old man."

"Nonsense, Captain. You're still a wrecking machine. I've seen the body cam footage from your prison op—very impressive."

"Thanks. Please, take a seat. What's on your minds?"

"Mostly it's Bev," Jericho said. "I'm just ready to get back to active duty."

I glanced over at Beverly. Her eyes were fixed downward.

"What's going on?" I asked.

She slowly lifted her gaze to meet mine.

"I'm pregnant," she said quietly. A tear slid down her cheek.

Somewhere in the back of my mind, I already knew. The signs had been there before the mission—her fatigue, her change in demeanor, her deepening relationship with that fleet officer.

"That's great news," I said, rising to give her a hug.

She held on tightly, and I returned the embrace. Then we broke apart.

"Thanks, Captain. I wanted to tell you both before the mission, but...it didn't feel like the right time or place."

"It's okay," I said. "How far along are you?"

"Two months and a few days."

"Are you kidding me?" Jericho said. "My cousin Lanita looked like a beach ball by now. I'm seriously going to have to cook for you and my future niece."

"Not sure that's a good idea," Beverly said, smiling faintly.

"Nonsense. My little niece is going to be a badass—just like me."

The two women locked eyes for a moment, as if mentally sparring.

Both of them worked well together when on assignment, but Beverly liked to remain distant and isolated outside of work. I couldn't blame her, sometimes the solitude was the only thing that helped keep a person grounded. Able to have a normal life outside of service and the hard choices one had to make on a day-by-day basis.

Before it could escalate, I spoke up.

"What are your plans, Beverly?"

She looked at me.

"I think I'll go home to London. Have the baby there with my parents. After that... I'm thinking about leaving the service."

Words failed me. I just nodded.

Jericho, however, found something to say.

"Why would you want to leave all this behind? You'll be bored to tears."

"Jericho," I said, giving her a pointed look. "I'm even thinking about leaving the service."

That hit them both like a bombshell. They stared at me—confused, stunned.

"Before either of you say anything, it's not official. After everything that's happened... I need to rethink my life. Maybe find a new purpose—something other than death and conflict."

Jericho shook her head.

"No, Captain. Unacceptable. All you need is some time off—get your head clear."

"Like I said, it's just something I've been thinking about. I probably shouldn't have brought it up."

Beverly reached out and touched my arm.

"It's okay to be uncertain," she said. "Honestly... I'm scared too. I don't want to leave the service, but I want to be there as my child grows. I want both—but I know I can't have both."

"I'm out of here," Jericho said, standing. "I'll talk to you both when the rocks clear out of your heads—or whatever medication they've got you tripping on."

"Jericho, wait—" I called, but she was already out the door.

"She'll be okay in a couple of days," Beverly said. "Besides, I should go too—before the nurse kicks me out for the night."

She gave my arm a gentle squeeze, then followed Jericho out.

I shouldn't have said anything. I should've kept my thoughts to myself—like I usually do.

I spent the rest of the evening flipping through stations until sleep overtook me.

***

The next morning, I was awakened by a nurse drawing blood. At the end of my bed stood Admiral Thadd, holding a stack of folders.

"I brought these for you, Jack. It's everything we recovered from Novick City—about Ethan and the experiments in the old mining tunnels. Believe me when I say I had no idea what they were doing."

There was no hesitation in his voice, no flicker of deceit in his expression. He was telling the truth.

"Why bring this to me now?" I asked.

"To hopefully mend some bridges," Thadd said. "Let me know when you're ready to talk."

Then he left.

And I just sat there.

Staring at the folders.

I already knew most of the truth—but inside those files was everything.

And still... I just sat there. Staring.

Chapter: Ten

A few days later, I was back on Earth—standing at the graves of my wife and daughter.

I placed a single rose on each and stood silently, letting the cold drizzle fall on my face.

The bite of autumn was sharp, but I didn't feel it. I was lost in memory—my daughter's first steps, her birth, my wife's face when she told me she was pregnant over Thai food.

"I'm lost," I whispered. "I don't see the path forward without you two. But after everything I've seen… I've decided to resign my commission. The war's over. Trouble's still brewing out there, but I don't want to be part of it anymore."

I looked at their names etched in stone.

"I thought I should tell you in person. It felt important."

I stood there a while longer, then turned and walked away.

I didn't know what the future held.

But I was finally free to find it—on my own.

Part: II

Chapter: Eleven

Six Months Later

Nothing good ever happens at three in the morning.
The dream that woke me began in the more active streets of New York. A cold breeze blew through, stirring up loose debris from the bombings. Everyone passed by without so much as a glance.
Then the world stopped. A bright flash blasted through me, and suddenly I was flying high, like an angel. Below, the remains of New York vanished beneath a mushrooming cloud.

In the dream, I felt no emotion—just a distant observer watching it all unfold. And then I woke, heart racing, but otherwise without any unusual physical sensations.

I knew it was a vision of the future. The bombed-out ruins were still there, even if nothing in the dream gave a clear sense of when it might happen. My instincts told me: soon.

M6 spoke in the back of my mind. "This is the second night in a row."

Even though M6 could read my thoughts through the neural link, I replied aloud. "I know. Activate the coffee maker." At least it woke me up early enough to eat before my shift.

"Not to alarm you, but I have an urgent matter to address before you sit down with your coffee."

"What could possibly be urgent at three a.m.?" I asked.

"Just before you awoke, someone placed an envelope under the door. Judging by the heaviness of the footsteps, there's a seventy-five percent chance it was a male."

"I take it the building's security cameras are still down?"

"You should've taken care of that personally a couple of months ago," M6 replied.

"I've been rather busy," I said. "Besides, the power grid hasn't been fully functional in this area for at least three weeks now."

"I could recite your activities from the last three weeks, but I'm sure the memory of those aching hangover mornings is quite vivid," M6 said.

"Here's an idea," I said. "I could've saved the city some power by shutting you off."

After that remark, M6 went silent. I got up and moved into the living room. The city lights outside provided just enough illumination to navigate by. At the base of the door laid a legal pad–sized folder.

"Low lights," I said, carrying the folder into the kitchen. I poured myself a hot cup of black brew and sat at the cracked glass table.

Inside was a single handwritten note: *We need to talk. Noodle bar, two blocks over.*

"Do you have an analysis of the handwriting?" I asked. "Judging by the awkward letter T, I hypothesize the note was written by Admiral Thadd," M6 said in response.

Why in the hell would he want to meet—and why the secrecy?

I still had three hours before I was due at the construction site, plenty of time to figure this out.

"Any instructions for the day?" M6 asked.

"Go through the news feeds. I doubt you'll find anything connected to my dreams, but check anyway."

After what happened in Novick City, I couldn't just dismiss the dream as meaningless.

Instead of fixing my usual breakfast—toast and whatever jam I had on hand—I decided I'd just get a noodle bowl at Kang Woo's. That was the only noodle bar I knew of within two blocks. And had to have been the one Thadd wanted to meet at.

***

The streets were dark and unusually cold for an early summer morning.

After the bombings, Earth's weather patterns had shifted. Scientists on the news claimed it could take years to return to normal.

I tried not to think about it. It was part of my ongoing effort to declutter my mind. I'd even made more time for moving meditation practices like Wing Chun and Tai Chi, followed by sitting mindfulness meditation.

The smell of cooking meats, onions, and peppers hit me a block before I reached the noodle stand.

There was an open seat beside a man in a navy-blue zippered jacket and a baseball cap. His build and the way he glanced over his shoulder told me it was Thadd.

I sat next to him, gave him a quick glance, and confirmed it. Kang, as always, greeted me with a slight nod and asked if I wanted my usual.

I nodded and a few seconds later a steaming bowl of noodles with shrimp slid to a stop in front of me. Wasting no time, I broke apart a set of chopsticks and dove in. Noticing Thadd's hat bore the Boston Celtics logo, I made mention to him about it.

"Not a very popular team around here," I said.

"Wife's from Boston. Never had much time to follow sports," Thadd replied. "How've you been, Jack?"

"Staying busy. Rebuilding the city is a huge project."

"An important one," Thadd said. "Ethan isn't dead."

My grip loosened on the chopsticks, and the noodles slipped back into the bowl. If Ethan was alive—and the executives were still under his control—it was the stuff of nightmares. It was also the confirmation I had been needing. Because up to this point I was just making assumptions.

"I need your help, Jack. Someone I can trust, outside the system."

"I should remind you—I no longer answer to you," I said, picking the noodles back up with the chopsticks and eating a shrimp-flavored bite.

Thadd turned on his stool toward me. "Article 12, Section 14 states that any former officer of the CEF can be reactivated by a superior officer."

I shoved a mouthful of noodles in before replying. "Last I checked, that only applies during wartime. We're still at peace, aren't we?"

"For now," Thadd said. "Jack, I'm not going to argue with you."

He reached into his jacket and pulled out a small clear cylinder, holding it out to me.

"All I'm asking is that you look this information over."

I took it, feeling its cool surface.

"What if I don't see what you do?"

"Then this was just a meeting between two old comrades sharing a meal."

"If that were the case, I'd have picked a better meeting spot. Tony's reopened a couple blocks from here—best pasta in New York."

Thadd stood and extended his hand. I shook it, noticing the smoothness around his fingers.

"Next time, then," he said, and disappeared into the dawning light.

I still had an hour before work, and with the data cylinder in my pocket, I knew I had to review it.

For months I'd had M6 scanning the news for any mention of Artran telepaths or anti-Artran protests. So far, nothing had suggested Ethan survived.

Whatever Thadd wanted me to see—it had to be conclusive.

And honestly, I couldn't resist discovering the truth for myself.

Chapter: Twelve

The most conclusive part of the files Thadd had compiled was a video showing the CEO of Greystone Mining Corporation speaking directly to the CEF High Council. In that dark and intimidating chamber, his voice echoed off the cavernous walls.

It resembled more a dystopian tribunal than a chamber meant to represent the dozen or so colonies of the Colonial Earth Forces.

"The Artrans cannot be trusted to keep the peace," the CEO said. "It has come to our attention that officers within the CEF have fallen under the influence of Artran telepaths. We demand a third-party investigation."

I didn't need to watch the rest. I knew right then and there—it was true. Ethan was alive and manipulating people.

"The rest of this evidence is compelling," M6 said. "Thadd tracked the corporate freighter that picked them up—before you sent the Insurgent code."

"I guess I don't have a choice," I said. "Ethan has to be stopped, especially if my dreams are foretellings of a future event."

"Thadd included direct contact information in the data. Do you want me to initiate communication?"

"Make sure it's fully encrypted—and do it."

Thadd responded immediately. He was already back in uniform, a grin on his face.

"I knew I could count on you, Jack."

"I take it you want me to investigate this solo for now?"

"You can pick up your gear in locker one-twelve at the nearby grav-train station."

"Any idea where I should start?" I asked, spotting my half-finished coffee still on the table. Even cold, it was bitter and strong.

"We tracked all the shipment crates. Only one unscheduled crate was sent straight to the Greystone Corporate Tower here in the city. We believe the nukes taken from Septis Four are housed in the vault chambers beneath the building."

"Speaking of which—did your investigation uncover where Ethan got those warheads? I never saw any mention of them in the reports before I resigned," I said.

"It took some digging, but apparently the CEF stockpiled a small cache just outside the city when it was first built—and then forgot about it."

I nodded, already mentally shifting toward infiltration. M6 projected building maps into my peripheral vision.

"Jack," Thadd warned, "you're completely solo on this. If you're captured, the CEF will disavow any knowledge of your actions."

"I understand. What happens once I confirm the nukes?"

"That gives me grounds to involve the council and launch a full investigation into Greystone Corporation. Let's see them try to deny where those warheads came from."

"Any way to counter Ethan's telepathy if I run into him?" I asked, taking another sip.

"There's a vial of Tetrasol in your locker. It can block telepathic influence—but it's not foolproof. As you already know, it failed to keep Ethan under control."

"I'll make this operation quick," I said. "Expect to hear from me within a few hours."

"Good luck, Jack," Thadd said, and the feed cut out.

"Go into stealth mode, M6," I said, watching the matte-black spherical droid phase out of sight. I was fortunate Thadd had successfully argued to the council that I could retain M6 and its stealth tech.

"Get us an air taxi," I added. "It'll be faster to reach the station. Also, pull up a list of Greystone executives living in the city."

"I have one match: Eugene Roger Corbin III, age forty-eight. Lives in the penthouse suite on Fourth Avenue, near the Corporate Tower."

"He's our first objective. His keycards should give us access to everything. How long until the cab gets here?"

"ETA five minutes," M6 replied.

Plenty of time to fix another cup of coffee and pour it into a to-go cup. As I poured, I noticed for the first time—my hand was trembling slightly.

Why?

"M6," I said, "run a bio-scan."

"Elevated heart rate and a spike in epinephrine detected. I recommend chamomile tea, not more coffee."

"No time for that. Where's the cab?"

"Just arrived."

The more I stared at my hand, the worse the trembling became.

Was I afraid?

And if so, why did my body react, while my mind remained calm—almost numb?

***

The trip to the ruined train station was uneventful. The cab driver waited while I retrieved a large duffel bag. Our next stop was the penthouse.

It was still early, and the city hadn't fully awakened. Fortunately, a heavily damaged building nearby had been vacated. I used it as a staging area to change into my armor.

"I've been observing the building," M6 said. "Most internal security systems are down. Employment files show there are four to five guards patrolling the building at all times."

"Thanks for the intel. I'll be back soon," I said, activating stealth mode and heading toward the target.

I waited a few minutes outside the main glass doors until an early riser exited. Slipping in unnoticed, I moved through the marble-tiled lobby and columns to the elevator.

A woman in tight-fitting pants and top held the door. I stepped in behind her.

It would've been safer to take the fire escape—but this was a thirty-story building.

She exited on the twentieth floor. I quickly pressed the button for the top level—but it didn't light up. Worse, the door closed, and I was headed back down.

Above the floor numbers was a slot for a keycard—something not in M6's file on the building.

It must have been a recent or well-hidden upgrade.

The elevator stopped again. Four fit men in business suits stepped in. The largest shoved into me.

"What the hell?" the man shouted, alerting the others.

All heads turned toward me.

That was it. The fat had just hit the fire.

I struck the big man in the chin with an open palm.

Chapter: Thirteen

The blood on the elevator walls wouldn't be quick or easy to clean—and forget about hiding four bodies. I hadn't killed any of them, but I was sure at least two would be eating through a straw for a while.

Accessing the elevator's roof hatch would take time, especially since it was bolted shut. My best option was chaos. Stepping into the hall on the thirteenth floor, I found a fire alarm and pulled it.

It didn't take long for the building to become a buzzing hive of activity. I was already racing up the fire escape to intercept Roger Corbin III on his way down. Unfortunately, a few people got in my way, and I had to shove them aside to maintain momentum.

By the time I reached the thirtieth floor, the fire escape door hadn't been opened. The way the doors were designed, you couldn't enter from this side.

"First responders are on the scene," M6 said. "I've tapped into their communications. They're aware of the bodies found in the elevator. Special Enforcers have been requested."

"In for a penny, in for a pound," I muttered, placing explosives at the door's edge. After running down a few flights, I detonated it.

The blast sent a thick cloud of white dust into the hallway. I pushed through it and entered a sprawling marble-floored living room, adorned with ornate statues and massive paintings—most depicting Napoleonic-era battles. I could tell by the bicorne hats on the officers.

The entire floor had been converted into one giant living space. A middle-aged man with balding dark hair sat in a wingback chair by the window, calmly sipping tea from a cup balanced on his lap. He looked directly at me.

Despite the door just having been blown off its hinges by an invisible force, he didn't flinch. No fear, no alarm. Just another sip.

M6 had already shown me his image—this was my target. I began striding toward him, only to halt when a dark humanoid droid stepped out from another room. A central blue light on its head locked onto me. It raised a rifle—and fired.

***

A few bullets struck my armor as I dove behind one of the large marble statues.

"Don't damage the art!" the man shouted at the droid.

I returned fire, but my rounds didn't seem to penetrate. Its armor was reinforced, and I had no armor-piercing rounds on me.

Tungsten-tipped bullets would've done the trick, but under the circumstances, I had to work with what I had.

I bolted toward a side room filled with more art and display pieces. Somehow, despite being invisible, the droid tracked me with uncanny accuracy. I took a couple more hits in the back as I moved.

"M6," I said, "how in hell is this thing tracking me?"

"This is an ECHO-series security droid by Omicron Technologies," M6 replied. "It's using a gravimetric imager to locate you."

"Explain," I said, ducking behind another statue as the droid stomped closer.

"Please do not resist. Surrender now and no harm will come to you," the droid intoned.

"How pleasant," I muttered. "Well, M6?"

"It's tracking you by the micro-displacement of gravity—your mass. The predictive AI fills in the rest."

"Suggestions?" I asked.

"Authorities have been alerted to your presence. Surrender to me now to avoid legal or bodily harm," the droid repeated.

As it drew near, I shoved a statue of a half-naked man toward it. With surprising speed, the droid caught the statue and prevented it from shattering. It bought me just enough time to flee deeper into the menagerie of paintings and statues.

That's when a second droid appeared in the doorway at the opposite end of the room. I was pinned.

"In theory," M6 began, "you could fool the gravimetric sensor by altering your mass profile."

"And how do I do that?"

The pounding of the droids echoed through the room as they advanced.

"Use the FAST tape. Then add materials to your armor. Distorting your shape should confuse the sensor."

"This is either the most brilliant or the dumbest idea you've ever had," I said, pulling the small roll of black tape from my utility tube at the lower back.

Nearby, I grabbed a small vase and taped it across my chest. Then I hoisted an old wooden chair with an opening large enough for me to place my arm through. So that it now rested on my shoulder and pressed up against my side.

I'm sure I looked ridiculous.

Standing fully exposed, I froze as both droids converged. With slow, deliberate movements, I watched—and to my astonishment, the trick worked.

One droid moved off. The other came close enough for me to stick an explosive charge to its back. As it stepped away, I hit the detonator.

The blast was immensely satisfying.

In the chaos, I slipped behind another statue and waited for the remaining droid to investigate its fallen comrade.

The balding man shouted from the far end of the room—probably over the ruined painting the blast had destroyed.

As the remaining droid passed me, I spotted a vulnerable joint in its lower back—thinner armor. I pressed the barrel of my weapon against the spot and fired upward.

The droid collapsed—knees first, then face-planting hard onto the marble.

Now it was time to deal with the man.

I shed the vase and the chair and deactivated stealth, letting him watch as I phased in—walking straight toward him.

Like a frightened animal, he froze.

Chapter: Fourteen

By the time the local authorities arrived at the penthouse, Roger Corbin was unconscious on the marble floor, lying in a small puddle of his own urine.

I hadn't had to beat a confession out of him. He told me everything I needed to know about the nukes—when they arrived and which chamber they were stored in beneath the corporate building.

The cops had no gear capable of detecting me, so I walked right past them and began the long descent down thirty flights of stairs.

One detail stuck with me: Ethan had been introduced to the board. Strangely, Roger couldn't recall what Ethan had discussed with them.

Just before the authorities arrived, I made a copy of Roger's keycards. Not that I could use them now—Greystone Mining Corporation would've already been alerted that one of their own had come under attack.

I was convinced I had enough evidence to report back to Thadd so he could launch a full investigation. Slipping past the media swarm and law enforcement in the lobby and on the street, I ordered M6 to contact him.

"Thadd is not answering," M6 announced.

"Keep trying," I said. "He's going to have to move fast."

Several minutes later, I stood beside M6 in the ruined building, watching the media frenzy unfold.

"I thought you should know," M6 said, "your attack is now making world news. A few reporters have even speculated that military agents are being telepathically influenced by the Artran."

Was Ethan among them, whispering in their minds?

"The CEO of Greystone is scheduled to give a statement shortly," M6 added. "Also, Thadd still isn't answering."

That was unlike the admiral. He might have been busy—but over an hour had passed. He would've sent some kind of message, especially given the delicate nature of this assignment.

"Do you want me to attempt contact through normal channels on an encrypted line?" M6 asked.

The sun had just begun to peek between the tall buildings, casting golden slivers of light across the city. I spotted a CEF gunship flying low over the streets.

"Do it," I said.

A few seconds later, the image of a disheveled-looking Thadd appeared in a projected visual overlay within my mind.

"Jack?" Thadd said. "Is everything okay? I haven't heard from you in months."

No. No, it wasn't possible. I tried to rationalize it. Ethan had manipulated me. It was him I met at the noodle bar. He'd lured me into something reckless—something that fit his agenda.

"Jack, what's going on?" Thadd asked.

I gave the mental order to M6 to disconnect the call.

"The CEO of Greystone is beginning his announcement," M6 said, then beamed the broadcast to me.

The man appeared tall and athletic, with dark hair and a clean-shaven face.

"Less than an hour ago, a board member of our company was attacked by CEF agents," he said. "For months now, it has become apparent to many of us in the corporate world that the CEF is under the influence of Artran telepaths. That ends today. I am calling for an outside party to launch a full investigation into the extent of alien influence within the CEF."

Once again, I had been tricked—outmaneuvered by Ethan. How long before they announced my name as the operative involved? Ethan wouldn't want me running loose and interfering with his plans—whatever they might be.

How could I turn the tables back on him? I needed to retrace my steps.

***

The walk back to the noodle bar took time, as the police continued closing down more streets. A second CEF gunship began circling overhead.

Those were what I tried hardest to avoid. It was possible that snipers on board were using enhanced scopes—perhaps even the same gravimetric sensors those droids used—to try and locate any Ghost operatives.

Several stools at the bar were empty, including the one where the fake Thadd had sat. Visually, I saw nothing that might offer a clue. But over the past couple of months, I'd experienced occasional flashbacks when touching objects—one more sign of my budding psionic abilities.

I sat down and placed a gloved hand on the bar, closing my eyes to try and force a vision.

Nothing. In the past, it had always happened spontaneously.

"Remove your glove," M6 said.

I hesitated, knowing the risk of exposing my visible hand to the few other patrons. But the chance of learning something outweighed the risk.

The varnished wood was cold to the touch. Almost instantly, I had a vision—a clean, well-lit hallway painted in soft off-white. The floor gleamed with polished wood. Doors lined the corridor, and then a painting came into view: a beautiful Victorian-era woman dressed in white, holding a small umbrella aloft.

The vision propelled me farther down the hallway, stopping at a Room. As the door opened, the vision abruptly ended.

A construction worker had bumped into me in the noodle bar, knocking us both to the ground.

I heard a few men laughing around the incident as the worker looked around in confusion, clearly unable to explain what had happened. I snatched my glove and left at a brisk pace.

The vision had been intense—like I was actually there, inside the moment. I didn't yet know which motel it was or where, but M6 had an idea.

"The painting you saw is a Sigo original. It was purchased by the Grand Plaza downtown for thirty thousand dollars."

At least now I knew where to go next.

"Admiral Thadd is making a statement to the press," M6 reported.

I paused, then gave the mental order to play it in my peripheral left-hand vision.

Thadd, dressed in full white uniform, stood at a podium.

"The CEF has determined that the recent actions against Greystone Mining Corporation were carried out by a former military operative, Jackson Howard Donovan. His motives are unknown, as are the full extent of his actions."

Thadd kept talking, but I stopped listening.

I was now a fugitive—wanted by the Colonial Earth Forces.

And with that earlier call to Thadd… they now knew I was in the city.

Special ops teams would already be on the move, hunting me down.

It was only a matter of time—either I unraveled what Ethan was planning… or I spent the rest of my life in a prison cell.

The Grand Plaza was a megastructure, just like all the buildings in the downtown area. The foyer and entrance were just as opulent as the Regency, with marbled floors and towering columns. The only difference was the abundance of trees and plants growing up through the center.

"What floor is the painting on?" I asked, watching a trio of women in short designer dresses head toward the bar. Judging by the upbeat music playing, there was probably a small dance floor nearby.

"It's on the one hundred and thirteenth floor," M6 replied. "I've also identified several exit points, including a map of the sublevel, which connects to the subway."

"Good intel," I said. "Now let's move. It's going to be a hike. How likely are you to hack into the local system?"

"It will take several hours at minimum, based on the algorithm they're using," M6 said.

"No money saved there, huh? Guess they like to keep their client list nice and secret."

"Agreed," M6 said. "Especially considering the dark history associated with this motel."

"No time for a history lesson. Heads up—ECHO droid patrolling the lobby. Come on, move! We can get into the stairwell before it spots us."

"I believe we're in the clear," M6 said. "The emissions from its gravimetric sensor didn't even sweep our direction."

"Fly up the shaft and expand your sensor range. I don't want to be surprised by another one of those things," I said, watching M6 ascend straight up the middle while I began the long climb, already breathing hard as I took two steps at a time.

By the time I reached the one hundred thirteenth floor, I had to stop and catch my breath.

"Since your resignation," M6 noted, "your cardiovascular fitness has declined, as has your muscular mass. Push-ups and pull-ups per week are below baseline."

"Thanks for the coaching. I'll keep that in mind. Now let's move—and don't mention my fitness again, unless you want your logic algorithms rewritten."

The hallway looked exactly like the one in my vision. A few feet in, the painting was on the wall. Now the question was—which door had Ethan gone into? There were about fifty along the corridor.

I removed my right glove and began systematically touching each door handle. It wasn't until I reached the last door on the right that a vision locked me in place.

***

It was nighttime, and I was standing in front of a modest house in the countryside. I held a sawed-off shotgun in my hand and used it to blow the door handle off for a quick entry.

Inside, everything was dimly lit. I heard the growling of a dog from upstairs.

I ascended the front foyer steps quickly. A young and very pregnant, dark-haired woman stumbled from a bedroom doorway, pistol in hand. She didn't have time to fully react before I smashed her in the face with the butt of the shotgun.

I looked down at her, the barrel of the weapon aimed at her unmoving body.

The dogs growling getting louder, followed by the sounds of scratching at a door. As the vision faded.

***

Had I just seen Ethan brutally attack Beverly?

"There is no public record of this event," M6 said.

The vision was strong and vivid. It had to have happened recently. Maybe the CEF had silenced the media.

Why would Ethan go after Beverly? If he had, I'd kill him myself.

"The door is now unlocked," M6 said.

I didn't hesitate. I flung it open and stepped into a small hallway. A bathroom was to the left, and ahead I saw a pair of feet on a bed.

Rifle raised, I moved into the room. All corners were clear. Beverly lay still in a navy-blue nightgown, hooked to a medical bag that slowly dripped something into her arm.

The left side of her face was swollen and discolored—greenish brown. That meant the assault occurred roughly four to seven days ago.

Why hadn't Thadd told me about this? If I'd known, I would've been even more cautious about Ethan. It might have changed everything.

"Her vitals are stable. However, a heavy sedative is present in her bloodstream. She won't wake for several hours."

"What about the baby?" I asked, still examining her body with my eyes.

M6 reported back, "All scans indicate it is healthy and unaffected by the drugs."

Relieved to know Beverly and the baby were alive, my eyes caught a small notepad on a desk near the closed balcony curtain. There was no visible writing, but a deep impression had been left on the top page.

Whoever wrote it had pressed hard. Tilting it in the light, I could make out one word: Kuroseki, and below it: 0300.

"I will begin running a search," M6 said.

Now I had to get Beverly out of here and somewhere safe. I didn't care if I exposed myself to the authorities. What mattered was her life—and the life of her child.

I reached out and gently touched her arm with my gloved hand—and suddenly I wasn't in the room anymore.

I was standing at a distance from a sunlit kitchen table. Beverly was there, feeding her newborn child. Soft morning light filtered through the windows.

Someone stood off to my right.

It was Ethan.

He observed me like a scientist might study a rat.

"You're right on time, Jack," Ethan said, flashing a smile.

Chapter: Sixteen

“What is this, Ethan? What have you done to Beverly?” I asked, stepping closer to the projection of him.

“Relax, Jack. There’s nothing wrong with her. She’s simply enjoying her new baby and motherhood. Thank you, by the way.”

“Are we talking in real time, Ethan, or what is this?”

Ethan tilted his head slightly.

“Did you not hear me, Jack? I was thanking you.”

“Fine. Thanking me for what?” I asked, my fists beginning to clench.

“You were there at the funeral—for my Barbara and Bethany. I really appreciate that, Jack.”

“So, your way of thanking me is by nearly getting me killed in Novick City? And when that didn’t work, you tricked me into committing a major crime. You realize both the police and the CEF are after me now.”

“It was necessary, Jack,” Ethan said.

“No. It wasn’t necessary. The Ethan I knew would have talked to me. I don’t know who this person is that you’ve become.”

“What I’ve done, Jack, has been to help you. Why do you think I went to all this effort? I kidnapped Beverly so I could learn more about you—to make sure you’re not one of them.”

So this was all about the Artrans and his paranoid theory that powerful telepaths were secretly pulling the strings?

"So your conclusion is that I'm *not* part of this grand conspiracy?" I asked.

"No," Ethan said, shaking his head slightly. "You've just been an ignorant pawn, helping play out their grand game. I'm trying to help you see the truth."

A short burst of laughter escaped me.
"Ethan, there is no telepathic Artran. Remember when we worked together in the intelligence department? Our *first* assignment was to investigate that very question. Do you remember it?"

"Of course I remember it," Ethan said, folding his hands behind his back. "That's exactly what makes it the perfect cover. They want us to believe they're incapable of such things—but we were wrong. They've been experimenting for generations, trying to unlock telepathy. And they succeeded. Not all of them—just a select caste. They operate from the shadows, manipulating everything."

"What proof do you have?"

Ethan looked away, then spoke again.

"Before the Omega Mirror stopped functioning, I touched— briefly—a powerful telepathic mind. I saw an Artran guiding humans into conflict. I saw Earth burning."

"The Earth burned, yes—but not because of humans. There's peace now between us and the Artrans," I said.

"That's what they want you to think, Jack. I know you can't see it yet, but you will."

I let out another short laugh.
"And how's that going to work when I'm behind bars?"

"You won't be," Ethan said. "I have several operatives in the room with you right now. Don't resist them—they'll bring you to me.

Together, we'll expose the Artran traitors. And don't worry about Beverly—she'll wake from this dream state in a few days."

That's when I felt a sharp tap on the back of my helmet——and the vision, or whatever the hell it was, came to an abrupt end.

***

I was still in the motel room, my hand resting on Beverly's.
Two soldiers stood in front of me, dressed in gray armor like mine and holding the same model of rifles.

And I knew a third was behind me, barrel aimed squarely at the back of my head. At this range, my helmet would shatter, and the bullet would punch right through my skull.

Ethan wanted me to come quietly—wanted me to be part of this insanity he was building.
He should've known better.

I sent a mental command to M6—one I never thought I'd use.

"Activate the EMP burst."

It was the only way I'd have a chance—disabling their tech and keeping them visible.

"Cautionary reminder," M6 said. "This will completely drain my battery reserves and disable your phasing ability until a hard reset is performed."

"I'm aware. Now do it," I thought slowly raising my hands from the bed to make it look like I was surrendering.

Then I closed my eyes—just in time for the flash.

Chapter: Seventeen

Even with my eyelids closed and the tinted shielding of the helmet's visor, I could still see the flash—at least partially. I didn't have time to wonder if it had stunned the soldiers.

In a situation like this, instinct and reaction were all I could rely on to stay alive. I was still breathing, Beverly was still alive, and I had a mission now—one of my own choosing. Ethan had made this personal, and I intended to bring it to an end, one way or another.

Twisting my body as fast as I could, my hands found the rifle of the soldier standing behind me. The flash had stunned him just enough for me to snatch the weapon away and drive the butt of it straight into his visor.

I watched the faceplate crack wide open as it slammed into his nose. His head snapped back, and the rest of his body followed—collapsing to the floor.

A couple of bullets struck me in the shoulder before I managed to turn and return fire—wild shots, but one found a weak spot. The second soldier flinched, which gave me the space to close the distance.

The third soldier was regaining his senses and trying to aim. I didn't give him the chance. I charged into the wounded one, using him as cover.

With the rifle at my hip, I fired point-blank into his abdomen. Something gave—the man offered no further resistance. I dragged his body forward, using it as a shield as the third soldier scrambled for a better firing angle.

I hurled the body at him to disrupt his line of sight. The momentary distraction gave me just enough time to rush forward, blade in hand. He managed to fire a few shots, and I felt the impacts in my lower body—but nothing felt critical.

Now face-to-face with the last soldier, I shoved his rifle barrel aside with one hand and drove the blade into the weak spot under his helmet's edge.

The soldier gurgled as he collapsed, hands pressed to his throat in a futile effort to stop the bleeding.

I rushed to check Beverly. A few stray bullets had come dangerously close, but she was unharmed.

No time to dwell on it—sirens were screaming, alarms blaring. The authorities would be storming the building any second, and this time I couldn't just walk past them.

From my utility cylinder at my back, I pulled a compact mesh bag, rolled M6's deactivated body into it, and slung it over my shoulder.

The hallway outside was chaos—people running for the fire exits. Elevators were useless, and the stairs were swarming. I had a plan.

Once more in the utility cylinder, I pulled out a compact grappling hook and rope. Forcing my way through the panicked crowd, I reached the stairwell and anchored the hook securely before tossing the rope down the shaft.

It didn't reach all the way—an eight to ten-foot drop remained at the bottom—but manageable.

I began sliding down, controlling the descent. At some point, I started taking fire. A few more hits slammed into my armor. Then I fell—hard—onto the floor below.

Pain surged through my right knee, nearly bringing me down. Gunfire echoed through the stairwell. Along with shouting and chaos.

Fortunately, most police units still used standard 9mm pistols.

I paused, breathed through the pain, and forced myself upright. Bursting through the crowds at the exit, I pushed toward the lobby.

More cops were waiting, weapons drawn. They opened fire, even with civilians scrambling all around us. Limping from the knee injury, I pushed toward the rear staircase that led into the sealed-off substation.

I heard the roar of a gravitronic engine outside—the CEF gunship had arrived.

That meant CEF soldiers would be coming next.

Each step down the stairs was agony. Normally, I'd pop a pain suppressant and push through, but there was no time to dig through the utility cylinder.

The station was dimly lit. I dropped into the tracks and forced myself deeper into the darkness.

With my helmet's night vision still disabled, I had to fumble for glow sticks. I cracked one open and pressed on.

I'd lived in New York for years, so I had a vague sense of where the tunnels led. What I didn't know was which ones had been closed off due to the bombings.

That was what I always relied on M6 for.

I picked a direction—east—toward the most heavily damaged part of the city. If I could get to the ruins, I could hide, regroup, restore my suit's phasing ability, and get M6 back online.

But M6 would need a power source. I hadn't heard any footsteps or pursuit. That meant they were regrouping and planning based on terrain intel—just like I would've.

***

I'm not sure how long I walked. Eventually, I found another access point, but a quick check revealed both stairwells were blocked with rubble.

Good.

That gave me breathing room.

Flickering lights greeted me in the corridor. I found a restroom nearby, kicked the door open, and immediately caught the strong scent of old bleach water.

Inside, I located a wall socket near the sinks. I set M6's body on the counter and plugged him in.

Next, I removed my helmet and chest plate. On the back of the armor, I accessed a small electronics panel and found the breaker switch—tripped during the EMP blast. I reset it.

From the utility cylinder, I retrieved a cable and connected it to the power outlet, beginning the recharging process for my suit.

I dry-swallowed two painkillers and inspected my gear.

Everything checked out—except the right thigh plate. The shell was cracked with a spider-web pattern. One or two more hits and it would likely shatter, exposing a weak point that might also cause phasing glitches.

Still—not the worst-case scenario.

As the pain meds kicked in and the knee pain began to dull, M6's lights blinked on. The connection slowly reestablished.

"This may not be the ideal time," M6 said, "but I'm receiving a communication from Admiral Thadd for you."

Should I take it?

He'd probably tell me to surrender.

And I couldn't do that.

I took a deep breath.

"Answer it," I said.

Chapter: Eighteen

The projection of Admiral Thadd beamed into my mind. I couldn't help but notice the day-old beard growth on his face, the slightly disheveled hair, and the sag of his eyelids.

"Jack, listen to me. We found Beverly. She's being taken care of. I've also ordered all forces to stand down for now."

All of this could have been avoided if Thadd had just told me she'd been kidnapped.

"Jack, I know you're listening. Please—we need to talk."

Finally, I gave in. "You should've told me. I would've at least known Ethan was coming for me."

"I'm sorry—truly. I wanted to tell you, but the High Council wanted to keep a lid on this until we had proof Ethan survived the destruction of the *Elminster*."

"You're using the High Council as your excuse now? That's not the Thadd I know. How many times have I seen you go against their so-called wisdom just to get the job done?"

Thadd blinked slowly and rubbed his stubbled chin.

"Those decisions were made during wartime. Things are different now. Politics and perception—those are the battlefield today."

I wanted to lash out at him—call him a coward—but at the same time, Thadd had reached out on an encrypted channel. That meant he was being honest, at least to some degree. Maybe even trying to help. But it was too late for that. The quicksand was up to my neck now, and I'd be damned if I let it pull me under.

"We've known each other a long time, Jack. That's why I'm speaking to you as a friend now. I need you to turn yourself in—step off the playing field so we can focus on finding who did this to Beverly."

"I saw him, Thadd. He tricked me into believing he was you. All this chaos—it's his doing. And now I know why."

"I'm listening, Jack. Tell me everything," Thadd said, leaning in, eyes widening.

"He kidnapped Beverly to learn more about me. To prove to me that Artran telepaths are real—and that they're influencing our political decisions."

"What was his proof?" Thadd asked.

"Ethan said that before the Omega Mirror stopped functioning, his mind touched a powerful telepath. Someone from a secret cabal. If that's true, he never told me at the time."

"He did report it," Thadd said. "The High Council labeled it classified immediately. A formal investigation was launched, and Ethan was part of it. But no concrete proof was ever found."

"Why wasn't I in the loop, Admiral?"

"Because by that point, you were leading development on the DIM-series droids and other black projects. You were in high demand. Ethan was capable, experienced—we let him head up the investigation."

"Captain," M6 interjected, projecting a map overlay in front of Thadd's image. "Our current position leaves us vulnerable to attack from two fronts."

"Any alternate routes?" I asked.

"Unknown. No updated tunnel maps exist following the bombings."

Thadd continued, "I know trust between us has suffered. But I need you to believe me now—someone is using you. Turn yourself in. Let me help sort this out."

"You've done a great job so far, Admiral," I said bitterly. "I'm finishing this. I'm done playing anyone else's game. If you want Ethan, he's at Greystone Mining Corporation headquarters—hiding. Cut the transmission," I ordered M6 before Thadd could respond.

"Why the deception at the end?" M6 asked. "Evidence suggests Ethan is scheduled to take the *Kuroseki* from the New Jersey spaceport to the Mars colony in a few hours."

"Misdirection," I said, donning my chest armor and helmet. "What's your current charge?"

"Five percent."

I unplugged M6, stowed him in the mesh sack, and slung him onto my back.

"Low power mode. It might be a while before I can charge you again. Let's find a way out of this place."

With night vision active and painkillers in full effect, I was ready for whatever lay ahead.

***

Thirty minutes into the shrinking tunnels, I was nearly submerged beneath a flooded section. Massive collapses narrowed the path—at times, I had to dive underwater just to move forward.

That's when I found her.

The winter and cold water had preserved her body for months. Her young face and long brunette hair floated out above her head like an angel.

At first, I thought I was looking at my daughter.

So young. So beautiful. I felt an overwhelming need to free her from this watery grave.

A massive steel beam had fallen from the ceiling and crushed her lower abdomen, pinning her to the wall.

If I could just get enough leverage...

"I strongly advise against this course of action," M6 warned. "Tunnel integrity is critically unstable."

"I have to free her," I said, gripping the edge of the beam.

"This is not Jennifer. Freeing the body will likely collapse the tunnel."

"The family needs closure," I said, straining.

"Once on the surface, I can transmit her identity and coordinates to the authorities."

Debris splashed down behind me. A small chunk hit the back of my helmet as the beam groaned and shifted slightly.

"If you die here, Ethan may use the nuclear warheads to attack a populated city. Do you want millions to die—knowing you were the only one who could stop him?"

Another piece of rubble struck my back. I looked at her face again. The cheekbones were higher than Jennifer's. The nose— narrower.

M6 was right. She was already gone.

And I was the only one who could stop the death of many more.

Without thinking, I reached out and touched her face.

"Goodbye, Jennifer," I whispered. "I'll see you soon."

I don't know why I said it. Nothing felt rational. Everything was running on autopilot.

"Your air tank reserve is low," M6 said.

A red warning light flashed in my lower-left HUD: Low Oxygen.

My armor's air reserves were limited—designed for brief space exposure or short underwater periods. Ten to fifteen minutes, max.

I moved past the body.

A thunderous crash echoed behind me as the tunnel collapsed. I looked back.

Only one direction remained. Forward.

***

The further I moved, the more the tunnel narrowed—until it dead-ended at a subway train, derailed and jammed in place.

The rear door was open. Ahead, two bodies lay face-down.

"Methane buildup detected," M6 warned.

"How far does the contamination spread?"

"Unknown. Proceed with haste."

I climbed into the car, stopping short as I saw them.

Dozens of bodies, all piled near each other—frozen in death. Victims of panic.

I had to step over them to reach the next car. The door was open. Another dozen bodies.

I didn't have time to analyze the scene. But I could imagine what had happened.

The gas had seeped in. Panic broke out. People pushed and climbed, desperate for breathable air.

But there was no escape. Just paralysis. Suffocation.

A traumatic death.

I moved through two more cars, then found a side door cracked open. I squeezed through and entered another tight tunnel path.

My red oxygen warning flashed faster now. A yellow toxic environment warning blinked above it.

Breathing was harder. Sweat poured down my back despite the cold.

"Toxic CO_2 levels rising," M6 said. "You must hurry."

I pushed myself harder, weaving through debris that pinned the train in place. Just as I cleared a final obstacle—

I saw them.

Tracers. Lights. Shadows.

A squad of armed figures was approaching from the far end of the tunnel.

"Well, shit," I muttered.

Chapter: Nineteen

The more I observed this group, the more I knew—they were not military or police. They had no cohesion. Several of them stopped to chat while others moved ahead.

Some paused when they found a body near me. I watched as they rifled through the clothing, taking whatever valuables they could find.

These were the worst type of humans: scavengers—destitute predators who preyed on the sick and the weak. Most were men, carrying sawed-off shotguns and flashlights.

Each wore a basic face mask connected to a small oxygen tank slung across their backs.

My vision was beginning to blur, and M6 was saying something, but I was in survival mode now. I knew what I had to do.

Grabbing a glow stick from my utility tube, I snapped it, shook it behind my back to avoid detection, and tossed it toward the far corner of the tunnel—back toward the front end of the train.

The noise drew attention.

"I think someone's over there," one of the men said.

Three of them fanned out toward the light. Two lingered farther down the tunnel, still deep in conversation.

That left one, still crouched near the body.

Creeping up behind him, I locked my arm around his neck in a full chokehold. He thrashed hard at first, trying to break free—then went limp.

Quietly, I removed his mask and oxygen tank, backing into the shadows to use the gear.

"Hey! What happened to Hank?" one of them shouted as the trio rushed back. "Someone took his mask and tank!"

"Who's there?" another barked.

They raised their flashlights and leveled their shotguns, scanning the tunnel.

I dropped to my knees, fingers fumbling with the oxygen hose. My plan had been to rig the tank into my suit—but there just wasn't enough time.

M6 was still speaking in the back of my mind, but I couldn't focus. Desperate, I tore off my helmet and took several deep breaths through the mask.

Oxygen deprivation is a cruel thing. I don't know how many breaths I got in before I heard the shotgun blast.

With the helmet off, I was completely visible—and completely vulnerable.

I hadn't wanted to kill these people. I hated scavengers, yes—but they weren't soldiers. They weren't combatants.

My rifle was still slung across my back. I went for the pistol.

A second blast hit me in the back—buckshot tearing into my armor. Two pellets grazed my neck and face. The sting was sharp and hot, but I ignored it. I dropped to one knee with a twist, raised the pistol, and fired.

One scavenger screamed and dropped, hands to his chest. My next two shots hit clean—one to each of the others' heads. They dropped without a sound.

The two men from further down the tunnel turned and fled.

Four bodies. Just like that.

The blood of the desperate now stained my hands. There was no washing it off. Only moving forward.

***

A few minutes later, I emerged from the subway tunnel, blinking up at the pale gray sky of early afternoon. Light rain drizzled onto my face as I discarded the mask and oxygen tank.

I should've been worried about snipers or cops waiting topside—but this part of the city was pure ruin. Once-proud buildings were nothing more than skeletal rubble.

The air smelled of sea salt—the harbor was close. M6 quickly pulled up a location map. We were several blocks from the nearest reclamation zone.

"Any chance of finding a working vehicle out here?" I asked via neural link.

"After months without maintenance or power? Zero chance. Your best course of action is to head west."

"I'm running out of time," I said. "It's already 0200."

"Then I suggest you walk briskly," M6 replied.

Instead of walking, I slipped into a sheltered spot among the debris and removed parts of my armor. The thigh plate was damaged, and I was certain the phasing ability had been affected by the shotgun hits.

From my utility cylinder, I pulled the last of the FAST tape and patched over the damaged areas. It wasn't much, but I hoped it would be enough.

The thigh plate took one strip. The backplate, however, had multiple impact fractures. I used the remaining tape to cover the spiderweb cracks and ran a phase test.

Functionality was unstable. One or two more hits, and the plate would fail completely.

I reassembled my armor and initiated a full phasing systems check. The power meter read 21%, giving me about forty minutes of phase time.

I began walking again, eventually reaching a cleared path where heavy machinery had once combed through the debris looking for survivors.

But I knew—by the time they made it this far, anyone still alive was already dead.

"I've detected a group of people ahead. At least a dozen."

"Police?" I asked, engaging stealth mode.

"Negative. No active transmissions. No CEF identifiers."

So what were they doing out here?

I crept forward and spotted them beyond a mound of bulldozed wreckage.

"More scavengers," I muttered.

They were laughing, showing off trinkets and valuables they'd just recovered.

Why is it in human nature to prey on the dead? I had no intention of hurting them—but I was going to steal their vehicle.

M6 highlighted a beat-up van to my right.

"Why that one?"

"It has an auxiliary battery pack. We can use it to recharge while flying to the New Jersey spaceport."

"Good call," I said, moving to the passenger side, which was concealed from view.

To my surprise, the door was unlocked. I slipped inside.

M6 began hacking the ignition system while I slid into the driver's seat. The interior was retro—analog gauges, a physical control stick. No holograms.

"The owner installed custom modifications," M6 commented.

What an idiot.

That's when I saw a group of four breaking off from the others—two men, two women—all armed with sawed-off shotguns.

"How much longer?" I asked.

"Unknown. The internal system is more sophisticated than anticipated."

"Not the answer I wanted," I muttered.

They were almost on top of me.

I stood, slung M6 over my shoulder, and crouched down between the driver and passenger seats, holding my breath as their footsteps approached.

Chapter: Twenty

I could really see their faces now. They were all so young—maybe a year or two older than Jennifer. They passed around the front of the vehicle and over to the other side, near the sliding door. I half expected it to be flung open, which I had prepped myself to burst through, but instead I heard a series of bumps against the exterior.

A large rectangular mirror on the right side showed me what was happening. Both young men had the women pressed up against the van, kissing them while hastily pulling off their shirts. The women, in turn, were tugging at the men's pants.

They'd come out here to hook up. If I'd taken a moment to notice the couch already laid flat and covered in sheets in the back, I might have figured it out sooner.

The hum of the power core lit up the interior.

"Got it," M6 said.

Slinging M6 down into the passenger seat, I threw myself into the driver's chair. There were a few murmurs from outside, but just as someone began to open the side door—

I kicked it into flight.

"An excellent execution of theft, Captain," M6 quipped.

"I'm sure it'll look great on my next résumé," I replied. "Set it to autopilot—I'll get us hooked in."

"Already done."

Storm clouds swirled around us as we slipped into the sky lane traffic.

"Twenty minutes to the spaceport," M6 reported.

I checked the internal clock in my helmet before removing it—0221 hours. Ethan was scheduled to depart at 0300. That left me less than twenty minutes to find a way aboard his ship. And under current circumstances, I knew the port's security would be on high alert.

I plugged my armor into the onboard port, then connected M6 to another. Green indicator lights came on—power transfer was underway.

"What options do we have for getting aboard that ship?" I asked.

"High probability CEF has deployed personnel with gravimetric sensors to detect phasing. You could attempt to go incognito."

"I've thought about that. You still have the alternate retina contacts in your storage bay?"

"I do—along with a false ID card and a fake bank access card. Be advised: the moment you use them, the CEF will be notified."

"I know. That's why we'll use it as a diversion tactic. Pull up a list of vendors making supply runs to Mars."

"Working on it," M6 said.

I got up and headed toward the back of the vehicle. Beneath the bed, I found a large backpack stuffed with wrinkled clothes and disc golf discs. I dumped it all out and stripped down.

Slipping into khaki shorts and a blue T-shirt with a faded band graphic felt bizarre. The clothing was so lightweight and loose, it barely felt like I was wearing anything at all.

The boots I had on would draw attention, but after more digging, I found a few pairs of flip-flops and sandals. Neither was ideal for running—or combat—but I figured the sandals would give me better traction.

They were a tight fit. The previous owner's feet had been a little smaller than mine, and my toes pressed into the edge, but it would do.

"I have a list of vendors delivering to Mars colony," M6 said. "None to the *Kuroseki* directly, but several to independent freight ships."

"That'll have to do."

Now all I needed was a sucker to use the fake bank card—just long enough to get inside and slip into the loading area.

Of course, as soon as the retina scan flagged me, every guard would be on alert. But with luck, the fake account usage would pull them elsewhere.

"We're landing in five minutes," M6 said.

I unplugged the armor—charge increased by about 10%—and carefully broke it down, stuffing it into the backpack.

M6 remained in the mesh sack, disguised beneath a pile of clothes. Too bad the droid could smell, he'd complain about the socks. That I was sure of. He had done so in the past. I wonder where that quirk was buried in his code—I hadn't checked.

I found a bottle of aerosolized body spray and hit the bag to cover the scent.

We landed. I slid open the side door and stared out at the throng of people funneling through the parking deck toward the elevators.

Now, which one of them was going to be the lucky winner today?

Getting into the spaceport wasn't hard. The lower levels were filled with shops and eateries for travelers to kill time. The problem was the checkpoint to the elevators, located dead center in the building.

That's where they'd check IDs and scanned retinas.

I was confident my fake credentials would get me through—at first. But a minute or two later, the system would flag me, and things would go south fast.

I took a seat at a bar next to two middle-aged women, animated in conversation. One had left her black-and-red purse wide open on the bar.

I ordered a club soda and subtly glanced inside. A small wallet lay on top. No one was looking. I slipped it out, opened it, and replaced the woman's bank card with my fake one.

Both were generic, red-and-gray plastic cards—standard issue under the centralized banking system. No logos, just numbers.

Card swapped, I downed the last of my drink and checked my watch—a simple analog model with a leather band. My wife had engraved the back:

"Time is precious."

I could still see her in a white dress, holding a cupcake with a candle lit just for me. I was on the couch in our first crumbling apartment. There were buckets on the floor catching leaks from the ceiling. The whole place smelled like vanilla from the candles she always lit. Her smile was so—

A hand tapped my shoulder.

I jerked upright, half expecting a soldier.

It was the woman from the bar.

"Are you okay?" she asked.

I hadn't realized I'd been staring into my empty glass, tears silently falling.

I just nodded, grabbed a napkin, wiped my face, and stood to leave.

They watched me go with concern in their eyes.

Hell, I should've been concerned too. That memory had dropped me into a spiral. I couldn't afford that—not again.

I checked the time.

Eight minutes left.

"In order to access the cargo loading area, you'll need to steal an access card," M6 said. "I've marked a target approaching the checkpoint now."

In my personal vision, M6 highlighted a young man in a gray-and-white port uniform, pushing a dolly loaded with boxes.

I watched him make a quick stop by the bar. The two women were still talking, and I feared they'd distract him too long.

But after a minute, he made a beeline for the restroom. I followed, watching him park the dolly outside and enter the men's room.

Two older men exited just as I walked in, leaving us alone.

The young worker was at a urinal.

I moved fast—wrapped my arms around his neck, kneed him in the back, and dragged him into a stall. He fought at first, but eventually went limp. I propped him on the toilet and took his access cards.

Generally, a choke like that left a person out for two or three minutes—plenty of time for what I needed to do.

I made a beeline for the checkpoint.

A quick glance back showed the bar now empty—the two women were gone. Maybe the plan would work after all.

Except—

"No indication of diverted forces to the bar," M6 warned through the link.

That was bad.

Worse? The moment the officer scanned my fake retina, I heard shouting from the direction of the bathrooms.

The checkpoint officer's posture changed. Her hand went to her sidearm. Her blue eyes locked onto mine.

The plan had always been a long shot. M6 had given it a 25% chance of success.

And now, the clock had just run out.

Chapter: Twenty-One

When a life-or-death fight begins, the adrenaline coursing through your body heightens everything. In my experience, it even slows down time. Granted, not enough to make conscious decisions about every move—but I knew exactly what my first strike would be.

Grabbing the collar of the female security officer in front of me, I yanked her forward into a headbutt—square into the bridge of her nose. I didn't need to hear the crunch to know it broke on impact.

Her body recoiled, hands flying to her face—exactly the opening I needed.

There had been a male guard just a couple of feet behind her. He'd already drawn his pistol and was trying to find a clear shot past her. I wasn't about to give him one.

I kicked forward, driving my foot into her midsection and throwing my weight behind it, sending her stumbling backward—right into him.

They both crashed to the ground.

I kicked her weapon away, then grabbed his. A sharp kick to the side of his head knocked him out cold—though I winced in pain. Sandals were not the right choice for this kind of fight.

The crowd around me had scattered. Now I stood, pistol in hand—a standard 9mm Glock, probably with 17 or 18 rounds. I didn't want to use them.

"Security is on full alert," M6 warned. "We will not be able to access the *Kuroseki*. However, I have identified a private freight vessel cleared for departure to the Mars colony. You might still be able to board it before they leave."

"Guide me," I said, sprinting toward the elevators.

I pressed the button. One of them opened immediately. Behind me, I could hear screams and shouts. More guards were on the way.

Once inside, I swiped the stolen access card and hit Level 13.

"Will I make it in time?" I asked.

"Apparently, the captain is running late. The ship is clear to depart once he boards."

"How about an escape route if this doesn't pan out?"

"The odds are not favorable, Captain."

"Fine. Then I'll make this plan work."

***

The doors opened into a darkened bay filled only with automated droids ferrying cargo. The vessel M6 had identified stood nearby, and I spotted a long-haired man—grey ponytail, slightly stumbling—making his way toward the ramp.

Using the droids and freight containers as cover, I darted across the floor. Just as the ramp began to rise, I grabbed the edge and flung myself inside.

"There's an access port a few meters ahead in the floor. You should be able to hide there until the ship clears the port."

"What's the crew count?"

"Typically four or five, but I've only detected three individuals aboard."

"Keep me updated. I need a breather."

The adrenaline crash hit hard. My limbs were shaky. My knee screamed in protest. I'd gone nearly 24 hours without proper rest, and honestly, I could've fallen asleep right there with my head propped against a pipe.

No time to dig through the pack. I'd deal with the pain later.

I must have dozed off for a few minutes when M6 buzzed in.

"We are now safely in jump space en route to Mars," he reported. "I've accessed the ship's internal systems. All crew members are on the bridge. You're free to move."

"How long until arrival?" I asked, lifting the hatch.

"Six hours. Unfortunately, we're bound for a minor colony on the far side of the planet."

"Any way to divert course to Athens Colony?"

"Not without raising suspicion. However, there are several routes we can take from this location."

"Good enough," I muttered, crawling out and stretching my stiff limbs.

I found a dark corner and searched my utility cylinder. A small roll of bandages helped me wrap my knee—not perfect, but enough. Once the pain meds kicked in, I reassembled the armor. Power level: 28%.

I found a power cable dangling near the bay's center and ran it to a corner obscured by plastic barrels—giving me a clear line of sight to the entrance in case anyone came snooping.

With both M6 and my armor charging, I set about rebuilding my rifle. I had the guard's pistol, but I'd need more firepower soon.

***

At some point, I dozed off again. The silence was almost peaceful— too peaceful.

"We'll be landing in five minutes," M6 said. "Your armor is fully charged. I suggest phasing out and preparing to disembark."

"I have to pee first," I said, disconnecting the armor.

"You may want to wait. The nearest restroom is by the bridge."

"No problem," I said, heading for a corner. "I can't fight if I'm distracted."

"Your urine will leave a scent traceable to you. I advise—"

"Too late," I replied, reattaching my armor. "Besides, scent isn't our biggest issue. I'm more concerned with reaching Athens."

"Three main options. First: planetary freight hoppers. No confirmed schedules yet, but they regularly run between colonies."

"They'll probably be under surveillance. What else?"

"Supply trains—used for heavy cargo—run at regular intervals. Less monitored."

"And the third?"

"Passenger trains."

I felt the ship lurch beneath me.

"Definitely not the passenger train. I don't want to risk hurting more civilians."

"Understood. I'll gather more intel once I connect to local information terminals."

"Got it," I said, freeing M6 from his mesh sack. He lifted into the air beside me. "I've always wanted to visit the colonies. Their engineering marvels, their scars, their stubborn survival—it's the stuff of Old Earth legend."

M6 replied to my statement, "Mars history is a fascinating subject, Captain. We can discuss it later if you like."

No time to think about, I thought with the shake of my head. When would there be enough time again?

The ramp began to descend. For the first time, I saw the red sands of Mars, sweeping across the plains. Dust gusted against the transparent energy dome overhead. Giant ventilation grates dotted the landing pad, keeping the air breathable.

Far-off mountains loomed on the horizon. There were no clouds. No animals. No people.

Two massive loading droids approached the ramp. I walked between them unnoticed.

"Something's not right," I muttered. "With what happened on Earth—and my presence aboard this ship—there should be at least a dozen CEF personnel waiting."

"Agreed. I've marked an entrance into the tunnels that will lead to the colony's lower levels. From there, we can find transport to Athens."

"Anything on military scans?"

I glanced toward another small freighter. Its ramp was down, and droids were unloading it too.

"No chatter about us. No alerts from Earth."

I still felt uneasy as we made our way to the tunnels. The droids ahead of us entered first.

The passage was long, dark, and filled with dust. About halfway through, I noticed something strange—particles began to move on my helmet visor.

Smart dust.

I'd walked straight into a trap.

Designed to stick, smart dust was composed of nanoscopic machines that clung to armor, skin, clothing—almost impossible to remove. It burrowed into creases and pores, making stealth useless.

There was no hiding now.

"Well," I muttered, "I should've seen this coming."

If this were a trap designed for ghost operatives, it was exactly what *I* would've set.

But who set it?

And what would happen next?

Chapter: Twenty-Two

INTERLUDE: ADMIRAL THADD

Location: Earth, **Colonial Earth Forces Headquarters, New York, New York**
Clearance Level: OMEGA-CLASSIFIED
Timestamp: 16:00 Galactic Standard

Admiral Thadd found himself walking across the highly polished, gleaming marble floors of the Colonial Earth Forces High Council building. He had been summoned an hour ago—and judging by the anxiety in the officer's voice who relayed the summons, this meeting was not going to be pleasant.

In fact, he half expected the Council to strip him of rank and assign someone else to clean up the rogue operative mess.

"Thanks, Jack," he muttered under his breath as he pushed through the large wooden double doors of the chamber.

The first thing one noticed upon entering the chamber was the sudden drop in temperature. It was at least fifteen degrees cooler here than in the main hallway.

It was also very dark. While you could make out the path ahead, the walls were shrouded in a dim blue haze.

To Thadd, it had always felt medieval. Of course, the entire chamber had been designed that way—to instill awe, fear, and respect in anyone who entered. He'd been here enough times throughout his career that the intimidation had faded.

Now, he just wanted to get this over with. There were more pressing matters that needed his attention, and frankly, this felt like a waste of everyone's time.

His footfalls echoed off the high ceilings as he approached the end of the walkway. He knew he'd reached it when he came to the guardrail, protecting anyone from falling into the drop-off below. Above him, a powerful beam of light shone down, illuminating him directly—making it difficult to see where the voices of the Council members came from.

A strong male voice began to his left.

"Do you know where the renegade is now?"

"I do," Thadd replied. "We know he managed to board a freighter outbound for Mars. We've narrowed it down to a couple of ships, and I've alerted our forces to where and when they might expect him."

Another voice responded—softer, but firm—from a different part of the wall.

"We understand you reached out to the rogue operative and delayed forces from pursuing him into the substation tunnels. Why?"

"This Council is well aware of Jack's service, sacrifice, and commitment to this institution. We owed him a chance to surrender. Not to be hunted like an animal."

The first voice cut back in, more impatient.

"And in doing so, you allowed the rogue agent to slip through our fingers and escape off-world. All in pursuit of this supposedly dead man, Ethan."

Thadd nodded slightly.

"We believe Jack is suffering from a mental breakdown. He needs our care."

A third voice now—gravelly, blunt, and louder than the others.

"You had your chance on Earth to bring him in peacefully. This rogue agent presents a clear and present danger to our operations on Mars. We want him removed from the playing field immediately, Admiral."

Such a cold response, Thadd thought. He'd hoped they might offer Jack another chance. Instead, they wanted him dead.

Maybe the long war had drained the Council of its humanity. He was surprised he had any left himself. So many friends lost. So many families shattered. He could still recall their names, their faces.

If not for his wife and newborn son, he might have become just as cold as these men cloaked in darkness.

"You are dismissed, Admiral," one of them said. He didn't know which one—it didn't matter. His thoughts had drifted back to his son, taking his first steps. It was the one thing that gave him hope. The reason he kept fighting.

Turning on his heel, he marched back down the walkway and out through the double doors—finally able to take a deep, calming breath.

Sorry, Jack. I tried, he thought as he stepped out into the light.

Chapter: Twenty-Three

At the end of the tunnel, I emerged into a large bay area filled with containers of all shapes and sizes stacked along the walls. A multitude of large freight droids moved about, loading items onto grav beds that were linked together, ending with a sleek, silver, bullet-shaped engine at the front.

A soft glow emanated from the dome-shaped object atop the bullet—the gravity generator. I recognized it instantly. Its purpose was to create an inertial damping field—a protective bubble that would counteract the extreme acceleration of the gravity train and prevent everything inside from being torn apart.

"I have identified the train we need to take," M6 said. "It departs shortly and is headed directly for the Athens Colony."

"What about the smart dust?" I asked. I had no idea how to deal with it, short of ditching the armor entirely.

"If we delay here any longer," M6 replied, "there is a near-certain chance you will be captured or killed. Remaining in motion significantly reduces that probability."

I didn't have the energy to argue. "Show me which one."

M6 highlighted a long train near the upper corner of the bay, close to another tunnel exit. Workers were currently strapping down a pair of cylindrical containers labeled *flammable material* at the rear.

Knowing I didn't have much time, I sprinted across the bay and leaped onto a middle section of the train, landing atop a stack of long, steel tubing secured in place.

A second later, I felt the rising pulse of the energy generator nearby. The hairs on my arms stood up.

The train began to move—slowly at first—through the tunnel, and then out across the open plains of Mars.

That's when the speed kicked in—fast, then faster, until M6 registered us traveling at nearly 900 miles per hour.

The landscape blurred around me, and I realized we were rapidly approaching one of the mountains I'd seen after first landing on the planet.

As we neared the entrance of an old mining tunnel, carved through the mountain. The train slowed noticeably—just in time for me to spot the gunship off to my left. Soldiers equipped with gravity packs leapt from it, descending quickly—straight toward me.

Shots rang out, pinging against the piping. If I hadn't ducked behind the metal tubing, I would've been torn apart. That much I was sure of.

"They've landed on the second car behind the engine," M6 reported.

"Who are they?" I asked, peeking over the piping. The soldiers were advancing fast. I wouldn't have long before they had me pinned.

"No visible insignias," M6 said. "Based on movement and tactics, I believe this is a special forces unit."

I fired a few shots while retreating. The next car back held two massive, dump truck-sized vehicles. The enormous wheels made for excellent cover as return fire erupted around me.

M6 displayed a crude overhead schematic of the ops team and the train. Two soldiers were flanking from the left, while one pinned me down from the right.

The following cart—the one with the flammable labels—wasn't far behind.

"M6, what's in those barrels?" I asked.

"The first is PlasmaClean F-7. The second contains GelIgnite R-9."

"I might have to play the lottery if we survive this," I muttered, squeezing off another burst of fire. My ammo was running low—one extra magazine, and that was it.

"I am not following your plan, Captain," M6 said.

I slid back behind the final tire of the truck and eyed the nearest barrel. A screw-valve sat at the base. I dove for it, twisting as fast as I could.

Bullets hit me—one in the back plate, another in the shoulder—just as the greenish liquid started to gush out. I ducked around the edge. A third shot clipped my other shoulder.

Then the mixture ignited.

PlasmaClean F-7 had a short burn life but burned hot. It would incinerate most contaminants—possibly even the smart dust clinging to me. But it might also roast me alive.

The trick—or at least what I told myself—was to time the burn duration. Sixteen seconds was optimal.

I counted every beat, steeling myself. And at sixteen, I ran.

I charged through the fire, blinded by flames until I nearly collided with the dump truck's rear wheel. I burst out the other side, coughing, armor scorched but still intact.

One of the special ops soldiers spotted me. He raised his weapon—but froze, just as I did.

The final cart—the one with the barrels—had detached.

It spiraled off the back of the train and smashed into the tunnel wall behind us, exploding in a spray of debris.

Then the train lurched upward unnaturally. We slammed into the ceiling of the cavern, chunks of rock and metal raining down.

"The inertial damper has been damaged," M6 warned.

We exited the tunnel in an uncontrolled free-fall into the valley below.

Instinct took over.

I hurled myself toward the thick chains securing one of the dump trucks and wrapped my arms around it like it was the last solid thing on Earth.

And then—

Gravity hit.

My body felt like it was being pushed against the weight of the entire planet. Every muscle strained. Every joint screamed.

How long could I hold on?

Chapter: Twenty-Four

The train didn't crash into the valley. Instead, it pulled out of the dive and continued hurtling across the valley floor. At some point, the inertial dampers kicked back in, and the pressure was finally lifted from my body. And I could relax my grip slightly from around the chain. I was still on the cart with the trucks, but my whole body was exhausted.

That's when I glanced back and noticed the soldier clinging to my booted foot.

I didn't hesitate. I grabbed the pistol at my hip and fired several shots into his grey, blacked-out visor.

The moment the visor cracked, he threw himself on top of me, knocking the pistol from my grip. Fists rained down toward my face, but I kept both arms free and deflected the blows with short, sweeping motions.

Then an opportunity opened—I trapped his left arm. My right hand slid down my armor to the embedded blade in my thigh plate. With practiced ease, I pulled it free and stabbed upward into the soft spot beneath his armpit.

The blade sank deep, and blood began to gush from the wound. The pain forced the soldier to roll away from me.

I was just rising to my feet when another soldier approached from the opposite side of the truck's giant tire and fired two shots into my chest. I heard the distinct cracking sound of armor plates giving way.

Still on my knees, I rolled forward and took cover behind the opposite tire, scrambling to my feet. I didn't know which side he'd come at me from next. I wasn't receiving anything from M6 anymore—either I was out of range or M6 had been destroyed.

No time to think about that now.

Moving cautiously around the outside edge of the tire to the front. With rifle raised, I caught sight of the other attacker as he was moving away from me. Taking a step in pursuit, that's when the inertial dampers failed again, allowing the massive force of the trains speed to pass through.

This time, I was slammed face-first into the giant tire, right up against one of the giant lug nuts holding the tire in place. As the G-forces increased rapidly. The visor integrity began to fail. At first it was a small crack right at my nose. That spread into a wide spider web across my entire vision. I estimated I only had a few seconds before it gave away completely. And the metal lug would come piercing right through my nose and possibly out of the back of my head.

Then, just as suddenly, the force vanished. I found myself flat on my back, staring up at the Martian sun. Every muscle ached. It felt like I'd done hundreds of push-ups and planks. Just moving took sheer mental effort. Either the inertial damper had kicked back on or the train had slowed.

The ops soldiers were clearly suffering too. I saw them helping each other up—and I didn't waste the opportunity.

Slamming hard into them while they were at the edge of the platform, I sent the first one—the one I'd wounded—tumbling off the side, disappearing into the plains. The other stumbled back, managing to stay on board, though he'd lost both his pistol and rifle.

I still had my blade.

I lunged straight for the weak point at his neck. But his survival instincts had kicked in. He blocked me, and I stabbed into his hands several times as he desperately tried to protect himself.

Then I switched tactics.

After one more feint toward the neck, I changed hands and drove the blade deep into the split seam at his side. With a quick jerk, I pulled the blade free and stepped away.

The blood flowed freely from the wound. He staggered, still trying to fight, but I knew he was already dead—he just didn't know it yet.

In a final act of desperation, the man stumbled toward me. With a simple sidestep, I let him collapse face-first onto the floor.

He didn't move again.

Afraid the dampers might fail once more, I climbed into the truck's cab through the passenger door, the window had been shattered through by something. That's when I spotted M6, rolling around the floorboard, inactive.

I tinkered with his core, rerouting what little power remained.

At last, I heard his voice in my mind again.

"Multiple damaged sections," M6 said. "I will no longer be able to propel myself in this current state."

"It's okay," I told him. "We're both alive. I'll take that victory any day."

"You appear to have sustained multiple injuries, including burns."

"I'm fine," I said. "I'm just going to rest for a bit. Let me know when we're near the city."

M6 may have responded, but I didn't hear it. Exhaustion pulled me under.

***

A few hours later, I was standing in the business district of Athens Colony.

Towering corporate buildings stretched toward the parasteel domed ceiling. The sun glowed overhead, bathing everything in a warm light. It all looked pristine. No trash on the streets. No graffiti. Everyone around me was clean, polished, and well-dressed.

Which made me look completely out of place.

I was wearing a tight black armor underlay, with a yellow construction vest Velcro on and a hard hat that wouldn't stay on straight no matter how I adjusted it. M6 was bundled in paper under one arm. It was the best disguise I could come up with.

I half expected to be greeted by CEF soldiers at the transport hub. But none appeared. My guess? They thought I'd died on that train.

It might take them days to find the bodies.

Maybe I'd just bought myself some breathing room.

If I didn't screw it up.

"Are you sure this is the place?" I asked M6 through our neural link.

"I have access to the public network. According to public profiles, the owners of this apartment are off-world on Earth for the next thirty days."

Perfect.

The residential district was arranged in circles, just like the rest of the city. Mars cities weren't like Earth's rigid grids. From the outer dome to the inner parkland, everything spiraled inward.

I took an elevator up to the 166th floor. A few people glanced my way, but no one said a word. I probably looked like a worn-out maintenance worker.

The hallway was drab—grey walls, no art.

"So, what's the plan to get inside?" I asked at the door of Unit 1300.

"Old A-200 model security lock. Just send an electrical jolt into the pad to reset it."

"Why the hell are these still in use?"

"Earth replacements are expensive. Most Martians prefer to engineer their own."

"Great. Do your thing."

I held M6 close to the door. A faint electrical pulse buzzed, followed by a click—and I was in.

The apartment was spotless. Everything was in place. It felt staged, like a demo unit, even though personal belongings were clearly present.

One wall was lined with paper-bound books. Some were Earth classics—*The Three Musketeers*, *Frankenstein*. Others were Martian authors I'd never heard of. Paintings hung on the walls too, likely local artwork.

The rumors about Martian pride and culture? Definitely true.

I set M6 on a circular glass table and unwrapped him.

"What access do you have now?" I asked.

"Only the public database. It's mostly women talking about recipes, shows, books, and their kids."

"I'll work on getting you fixed up. First, I need a shower."

"Water is rationed. Only a certain amount is allocated per household."

"No problem," I said, already stripping down. "Five minutes, tops."

***

The water felt like heaven at first—hot, cleansing. Blood, grime, and stress washed away. But my raw skin, burned in places, flared painfully in the heat.

I clenched my teeth and kept scrubbing.

Then I closed my eyes under the spray—and I saw it.

Another vision.

Bodies of humans and Artran warriors littered the business district. The Artrans looked alien as ever: birdlike builds, long springy legs, leathery skin. Their branding—etched into their flesh—told their life stories. One, near me, bore the five-star cluster of an honor guard.

Then it came—a flash deep within the city, like the one I'd seen on Earth. A nuclear blast.

Everything vanished.

I awoke on the shower floor, cold water spraying over me.

Ethan couldn't have sent that vision. He didn't know I was alive.

No—this was another *real* vision. Like the one in Novick City.

And if it was true...

Then I didn't have much time left to stop him.

Chapter: Twenty-Five

For the next two days, I scrounged the city for components to repair M6 and salvage whatever I could of my armor. Most of the plates had cracked and were vulnerable to even small-caliber gunfire. The phase ability was permanently disabled.

I had the knowledge to rebuild the armor, but not the time or resources—not with Ethan on the move. And it was becoming painfully obvious that whatever I saw in that vision was quickly becoming reality.

With M6's full capabilities restored, he was able to hack into the local security channels. He learned that the new Artran ambassador was set to arrive on the planet within the next twenty-four hours.

Security was on high alert. Protests outside the Artran embassy were growing louder, angrier.

M6 spoke aloud, "I've discovered a recent murder report matching the details of the ones in Novick City."

"Any details about where the victim worked?" I asked.

"The train hub. Night shift supervisor overseeing the manifest."

Why would Ethan kill someone like that? With his telepathic ability, it should've been easy to manipulate the person into compliance. So, what was he missing? After all, Ethan had easily manipulated me into believing I was talking to Admiral Thadd.

"Can you access the autopsy report?"

"No," M6 replied. "But if you install a security spike behind their firewall, it would be simple."

"I can't just walk in there. Dead or not, my face alone would trip every alarm."

"I have an alternative," M6 said. "While monitoring the channels, I discovered a thriving black market for military tech. I've made several discreet inquiries and located a vendor claiming to have Ghost Recon armor."

"That's not possible," I said. "That tech is heavily regulated and confidential."

"And yet we've seen private contractors using it," M6 noted. "It may not be official military issue—possibly a prototype or reverse-engineered design."

"And how am I supposed to pay for this?"

"While searching the apartment, I discovered a hidden wall safe behind one of the paintings. Based on the owner's financial records, it likely contains several gold bars."

"Might as well add grand larceny to my list of charges. Do you at least know the combination?"

"I've narrowed it down to several possible codes."

M6 guided me to a painting in the bedroom. I couldn't tell what it was supposed to depict. Honestly, it looked like someone had just thrown red and orange paint at a canvas and scribbled some unreadable initials.

Behind it: an old-school wall safe with a combination dial. Classic.

"Seriously? A wall safe behind a painting? How original."

"What's the first combination I should try?" I asked.

"We'll begin with the most probable one," M6 said.

"How many are there?"

I waited.

"Two hundred and sixty-five million."

I shook my head. "I'll try a few. Then I'm drilling through the lock."

***

A few hours later, I was in the business district at night, standing outside a neon-lit nightclub. Hundreds of people passed by in the cool Martian air.

After drilling through the safe, I'd found six gold bars. M6 immediately contacted the black market dealer. We offered two. He countered with four. We settled at three.

Now here I was—three gold bars in an old gym bag slung across my chest.

A large, muscle-bound man with a shaved head and thick brown beard approached the club's entrance. M6 had given me the passphrase.

"Nick invited me."

The man grabbed my shoulder and silently led me inside. Even though the sun had only just set, the place was already packed.

Men and women of every race and ethnicity danced across a glowing floor under strobing lights. Holographic dancers looped overhead, shifting with the music. The bass thumped so hard it felt like a shockwave through my body.

We skirted the dance floor and passed a long bar before going through a side door that required a keycard. The man led me up carpeted steps to an upper floor with a panoramic glass wall overlooking the dance floor.

There, sitting on a plush couch flanked by two blonde women, was a sharply dressed man in a white suit. Mid-40s, dark hair, and a carefully trimmed beard. Blue eyes fixed on me as his bodyguard set the gym bag on the table.

"Take the girls down to the club," the man said. "Make sure they get whatever drinks they want."

The women disappeared with the bald man, leaving me alone with the dealer—Nick, I assumed.

He wore a chrome-plated pistol in a shoulder holster. Casual. Confident. Dangerous.

"I've been looking forward to this," Nick said as he unzipped the bag and examined one of the bars.

"Earth-minted. 1940s era," he said. "A pleasant surprise."

"What about the armor?" I asked.

Nick smiled and zipped the bag closed. "Of course. Follow me."

He gestured toward a wall. I saw no seams, no obvious hidden doors. Then he knocked on it—solid. Still nothing.

Then he pulled a small remote from his pocket, pressed a button, and reached through the wall like it was a hologram. Then he stepped inside.

I followed.

Inside was a weapons vault. Rifles, pistols, explosives, and armor lined the walls—each piece perfectly displayed. Illegal beyond measure.

Nick stood beside a new set of Ghost Recon armor—sleek, dark, and etched with the Omicron Technologies logo. Judging by the small lump beneath the shoulders, I think it was equipped with a gravity pack. Like the special ops soldiers had used to transport over to the moving train.

"How did you get this?" I asked.

He shrugged. "This is what I'm offering. Deal or no deal."

"Deal," I said. I didn't want to imagine what would happen if I refused.

"I do have one more request," I added.

Nick's smile widened.

"What kind of weapons and ammo can I get for one more gold bar?"

I'd hidden a fourth bar in my waistband, just in case.

Nick led me to a weapons wall. "Client's choice."

Chapter: Twenty-Six

After acquiring the new Ghost Recon armor, I stuffed it into an oversized duffel bag, along with the weapons and ammo I'd purchased, and set off through the business district toward one of the closest police stations.

M6 had been right — we needed more intel. Failure here meant the death of millions.

Finding a nearby public restroom, I slipped inside, found a "Closed for Maintenance" sign, and locked the multi-stall room for some privacy while I changed. The temptation to put the armor on back at the club had been great. I'd wanted to test it — make sure everything functioned correctly, but mostly because I felt safer in it. There was no telling, though, if security or the CEF were scanning for phased individuals using gravimetric sensors.

So far, there was still no public word about the grav train incident, but I was certain official reports were circulating. Hacking the police station remained our safest option.

Tying the last of my boot's laces, I stood and placed the helmet over my head. Everything darkened at first, tinted by the visor, then gradually powered up.

On my wrist console, I typed in the frequency M6 and I had agreed on earlier — the neural link range was too far now.

"Are you there, M6?" I asked.

The response came back, barely audible. "There is a problem."

"Explain," I said, already debating whether to remove the armor.

"A few seconds ago, one male and one female entered the premises. So far, I've been unable to get a full facial scan — they're… fully entwined with each other."

I sighed. "Did the apartment profile mention any kids?"

"One daughter. According to her profile, she's still attending university on Earth."

"Stay hidden. But if they alert the police, head to the backup location. I'm installing the spike."

"Understood."

"If it's not one thing, it's another," I muttered. If the daughter had returned early, it meant our safe house was compromised. She'd notice quickly that things had been moved, clothes rifled through, and the bathroom used.

The apartment had been absurdly clean when I arrived. Too clean — like they'd never lived there at all.

Standing before the mirror, I activated the phase module. My reflection vanished. I stepped back to get a full view — everything seemed to be functioning correctly.

The idea that corporations like Greystone and Omicron had their own versions of CEF Ghost Recon suits was deeply unsettling. What did they need them for? Espionage? Sabotage?

I stopped myself before I spiraled. I didn't have time for rabbit holes.

I unlocked the bathroom door and exited cautiously into the street, keeping low and using cover where I could on the way to the police station.

Eventually, I stepped through the front doors and into a large waiting room filled with rows of plastic chairs. People sat silently, waiting. At the back wall was a parasteel window and, to its left, a thick, handle-less metal door.

A black woman appeared at the window and called, "Number 323. Last call for 323."

An older couple stood and helped each other to the window.

I edged closer to the metal door, waiting. Eventually, a young female officer in red, black, and orange opened it. She held it wide just long enough for me to slip through.

Beyond was a room full of desks. Officers bustled, working at terminals or assisting civilians.

I hugged the perimeter and worked my way to another door that led into a polished hallway. I'd memorized the route, thanks to blueprints M6 had pulled before I left.

Down one level, two officers exited a keypad-locked door. I slipped in behind them, catching the door before it shut. Another hallway. This one was bare concrete. No marble. Each room had a keypad and a placard: *Armory. Records. Weapons Range.*

At the far end — *Server Room.*

It was eerily quiet. I didn't know how long I'd need to wait for access.

Then M6 pinged.

"CEF forces have arrived at the apartment. Admiral Thadd is with them. They're sweeping with Gravimetric sensors. I cannot escape."

How? How had they found us?

If they captured M6, it was game over. Every encrypted file, tactical plan — all compromised.

Still, if I installed the spike, I could remotely access critical intelligence. If I rushed to save M6, I might lose everything.

Painful as it was, I made the call. M6, despite his companionship, was a tool. Like the armor I wore.

Good luck, M6, I thought, flattening myself to the wall.

Several minutes passed. Then an officer approached and entered the server room. I noted the code: 400827.

When they left, I slipped inside.

The room was packed with routers and CPUs — outdated models jury-rigged together. I'd seen this setup before — in older colonies. These units were running hot, likely at maximum capacity.

I found a newer console compatible with the spike.

Spikes were advanced tools — intelligence-grade tech that infiltrated encrypted networks. Once installed, they melted into the circuit board, becoming undetectable. After a few days, they degraded and left no trace.

The black market had versions of them now, which meant corps were using them too.

I shook the thought away and inserted the spike. It slid into the port, hissed slightly, and began to dissolve.

Done.

I turned and left the server room.

Halfway up the stairwell, a message scrolled across my HUD: *We have M6, Jack. Let's talk. — Thadd*

I stopped cold.

Losing M6 was a blow, but I could continue without him. The real question was — how had Thadd found us?

Cautiously, I opened an encrypted channel.

Thadd appeared — sitting in the apartment kitchen. Clean-shaven, pristine uniform, perfectly pressed. This was the Thadd I remembered.

"Thanks for calling, Jack," he said. "I won't try to convince you to turn yourself in. But I do have someone here you'll want to hear from."

He stood aside. Beverly took his place.

Her dark hair was a mess, and there were tear tracks on her cheeks. "Jack," she said, her voice trembling. "Thank you for saving my life on Earth. That's twice I owe you now, Captain."

She leaned closer. "I know you think you're doing the right thing, but…you're having a breakdown. It all feels real — but it's not. Please, Jack. Let us help you."

My heart sank.

Beverly — next to my wife — was the person I trusted most.

And Thadd had turned her against me.

I tried to hold on. *She must have seen the evidence. Surely, she knows what I'm doing is right.*

Unless…

What if she was right?

Was Ethan even real? Had I twisted everything in my mind?

I had to find Ethan. That was the only way to know.

"Jack, please," she begged, her voice cracking. "Come to me. Let's figure this out together."

I finally spoke. "Beverly… get off Mars. Ethan has nukes here. I saw it — in a vision. I can stop him."

She shook her head. "No, Jack. You *can't*. Because he's already dead. The CEF recovered Ethan's remains. I've seen the reports. He died with the executives onboard the *Elminster*."

No.

I had seen Ethan. Spoke with him. This had to be a lie.

"Come to me, Jack," she whispered. "Please…"

I couldn't look at her anymore. Her tears reminded me too much of my daughter.

I shut my eyes. Slowed my breathing.

Then a chime. A new message on my HUD:

Please open the download.

The file — from earlier. A massive data transfer from an unknown source.

I tried to respond. The return signal failed.

Back in the kitchen, Beverly had left. Thadd sat in her place again, still talking.

I no longer cared what he said.

He had turned the last person I trusted into a weapon against me.

There was only one path left. Find Ethan. End this.

I climbed the rest of the stairs and exited the building.

The download waited.

I had no idea what it was.

But my gut said it mattered.

And I always listened to my gut.

So, I confirmed the download.

Chapter: Twenty-Seven

I was sitting behind two large trash containers when the download completed. During that time, I kept wondering how Thadd had found me. I still had no firm conclusions—just speculations bordering on extreme paranoia. Things like tracking implants, hypnosis, or even telepathy. I even tried to remember the last time I'd visited a dentist.

Was it possible one of my fillings had been replaced with something the CEF could track? If that had truly been the case, then M6 would've detected it.

A new message dinged, followed by a line of text scrolling across the visor: *Still adjusting to the new environment.*

What did that mean?

Then the idea struck me like a hammer to the head—had M6 downloaded himself into this new armor? Was that even possible?

There was so little I knew about it. Using the wrist console and verbal commands, I pulled up information about the system's specifications.

To my surprise, I discovered that the armor had a compact, quantum-layered memory array that supported up to 12 zettabytes of dynamic storage. This was very similar to the drive installed in M6. Was it possible the Omicron Corporation had plans to incorporate a sophisticated AI system into the armor?

The 12-core photonic neuromatrix was another sign that they definitely had such intentions. It was more powerful than the 10-core I'd used for M6.

"I have analyzed the spike you placed in the system," M6 said through the helmet's headset. It was obvious now there was no longer a neural connection between us.

"I'm glad to hear your voice, M6," I said.

"Let's get down to business," he replied. "I estimate that you have far less time to find those nukes than anticipated."

"What's changed? The Artran ambassador isn't here yet."

"That's exactly what we were led to believe. The ambassador has been here for days, hidden away in the embassy with his retinue. I now have access to all files in the police headquarters."

"Then why announce his arrival publicly? What's the point?"

"Because the Artran Chancellor himself is coming to Mars to sign the finalized peace agreement."

"This is not good news. When does the Chancellor arrive?" I asked, getting to my feet.

"In four hours."

That had to be when Ethan would strike—at the peace signing. It wasn't a perfect theory, but it was the best I had until more information surfaced.

"We need to find the nukes and disarm them—fast. What clues does the autopsy give us?"

"For one, a possible reason why Ethan killed the man. It appears the worker had a tumor forming in his prefrontal cortex. An operation was scheduled to remove it—until his untimely death."

"Could the tumor have blocked Ethan from manipulating him?"

"Hypothetically, yes," M6 said. "As for the familiar puncture in the back of the skull, I still have no clear explanation."

That puncture wound had bothered me since Novick City. It made no sense, not with anything I understood. But Ethan had a reason—and who knew what twisted, delusional purpose it served.

I took a deep breath and refocused.

"Where was the body found?" I asked.

"The Hub," M6 answered. "He was working on a loader droid that had malfunctioned."

"Then I guess we're heading back to the Hub," I said, peering out at the bustling city streets through the alleyway. The Hub—where I'd arrived at the Athens Colony—was a busy place. Mostly droids moved about, but there were a few humans performing maintenance or overseeing operations.

"One more thing, M6. It's been eating at me—how did Admiral Thadd find us?"

"I still have no idea," M6 replied. "But I've plotted a route to an above-ground lift platform. It'll get you back to the Hub quickly. I also have the ID of the loader droid in question."

I set off at a brisk pace, following the red-lined path M6 had laid out in my visor. I moved around crowds of people until I reached the facility housing the distribution point for this level.

"Do we know what freight the lifter was handling?"

"It came from the *Kuroseki* ship. But the crate ID is missing from the report."

"Of course it is," I muttered, watching construction trucks glide past me.

The terminal was alive with activity, much like the Hub below. Droids and humans moved in an orchestrated chaos.

"You're looking for unit LL-0096605."

"This is going to take a while," I said, scanning each droid ID I came across. "This would go a lot faster if you still had a body, M6."

"I agree. Though I look forward to the new and improved version you'll build for me. By the way, this armor's processor uses zero-latency positron tunneling. Quite an upgrade."

"Fascinating. Now help me find this droid."

"Already on it," M6 said, just as a pair of small black sphere devices zipped past my head and swarmed the bay.

"What the hell was that?" I asked, gripping my rifle tighter.

"Finder spheres. Prototype tech built into the armor—miniature phasing drones that scan crowds for specific targets. And there—it found the droid."

A bright green outline appeared in my visor. I followed it to a loader droid lifting construction piping off a grav train.

I'd worked on these models in my youth. I knew exactly where the leg panel was. Popping it open, I pressed the red button to pause it in place.

With time on my side, I removed my left glove, exposing my bare hand. I touched the cold, smooth metal and closed my eyes, reaching out with my mind the same way I had before.

Seconds passed. Nothing.

Then I opened my eyes.

Only to find myself staring down at a begging human man, lying on his back.

"Please...don't kill me," he said, voice trembling.

Looking down at my hands, I saw I held a crudely made shiv—razor-sharp at the tip.

Others stood nearby. Their vacant stares told me they weren't really *seeing*.

I was the killer.

And with mechanical certainty, I stabbed the man several times in the stomach.

Chapter: Twenty-Eight

Blood pooled around the body as the worker desperately tried to crawl away. I wanted to stop myself from what I knew was coming next, but I was unable.

The blood-dripping shiv in hand, I dropped one knee into the man's back and drove the point up into the base of his skull. Before standing, I heard Ethan's voice say, "Let's see them use your corpse against me now," followed by a soft chuckle.

Then I wiped the blood off the shiv on my shirt. Even though I couldn't control my actions, I now found myself looking at the crate the droid had been carrying. The number *2557* was marked in the upper left-hand corner in large red lettering.

There were more numbers, but something knocked me out of the vision.

Blinking a few times to orient myself, a bullet pinged off the loader droid in front of me while M6's voice reported in my ear.

"You're under attack. You need to move—now," M6 said, louder than usual.

Dropping and rolling beneath the grav train, I again felt the hair on my body stand up—the telltale ant-crawling sensation of being near a powerful electromagnetic field.

When I came out of the roll on the opposite side of the train, I had dodged one line of fire—but found myself in another.

The bullets that came at my chest were deflected by a shimmering silver field that quickly faded. That's when I noticed a new indicator in the lower right corner of my display: an outline of a figure with arms and legs spread wide, with a dim glowing bar wrapped around it. Likely a deflector shield status. It wasn't very bright, which meant it wouldn't last long.

More bullets struck as I ran. The shield indicator vanished, meaning the next hits would go directly into my armor.

Somehow, I'd been found—and surrounded.

With a glance around, I saw all the facility doors closing. I was being locked in.

"M6," I barked. "Can you triangulate the shooters?"

"Working on it. One shooter is stationary in the control tower. Two others are sweeping around you—trying to pin you in the center."

"Not happening," I said, climbing into a floating truck. Bullets clanged into the frame as I powered up the vehicle and floored the accelerator.

My target: the control tower.

Workers dove for cover. A few of the slower loader droids were hit as I rammed the truck into the circular building.

The windshield held, so I shot it out myself and climbed onto the hood. The truck now blocked the entry to the tower, giving me a chance to take on the sniper one-on-one.

I darted up the concrete stairs two at a time. Everything was quiet in the control room. The attacker wore Ghost Recon armor— and was nowhere to be seen.

He could've jumped out the shattered window, but my gut told me otherwise.

"The gravimetric sensor shows nothing," M6 said.

The armor had one of those built in? Was it designed to hunt other Ghost operatives?

No time for questions.

I fired in a sweeping arc—floor to ceiling, left to right. A waste of ammo, but effective.

Bullets struck something clinging to the ceiling. I refocused fire until the attacker dropped down and knocked my rifle away—even though it was still slung to my body.

My visor shifted to a black-and-white gravimetric mode. It highlighted the enemy in a white outline against a darkened background.

Everything became harder to identify.

Only when the attacker raised their pistol did I fully recognize it.

My instincts took over. I lunged, pushing the barrel away with my left hand while smashing my right fist into the helmet.

It didn't injure them, but it jarred them long enough to try disarming them—and go for my knife.

They moved with expert precision, letting my fist graze past their helmet before slamming into me. We crashed against the wall hard.

My armor cushioned the blow, but the impact knocked the breath out of me.

I still gripped their wrist, but in the black-and-white haze, I'd missed the pistol. The attacker went on the offensive. Knees, elbows—brutal, relentless. I had to let go of their wrist to shield myself.

That's when the shots came—point-blank into my chest.

This armor held for now. But I had no idea how much more it could take.

I shoved forward in desperation, tackling the attacker to the ground.

Vision blurred, but I knew where they were. They landed first. I followed through.

I latched onto their ankle, while getting up and then I stomped downward with my heel, targeting weak points. Twice I landed solid strikes, but they twisted free, rolled to hands and knees, and mule-kicked me in the chest.

I flew backward into a console by the window.

Through the murky visual, I saw them grab something off the ground, probably the pistol.

I pulled mine faster. My shots hit. I couldn't tell where until I heard a scream—and the figure collapsed.

I followed M6's instructions to open the bay doors. That's when a bullet struck the back of my helmet.

I staggered forward from the impact, but let the momentum carry me. I rolled over the console and out the window.

It was only a two-story drop, but when I landed, my knee exploded with pain.

Adrenaline didn't dull it. It flared.

I don't know how long I lay there, clutching my leg. Bullets tore into the ground around me.

I rolled to cover—one of the four-legged loaders. Not much, but it bought me a breath.

"M6, options?"

"There's a control panel beneath the loader. Insert your last spike—I can take over."

"Use it as moving cover?"

"Precisely. But what's our destination? Did your vision provide a lead?"

Bullets ricocheted. I shot open the panel and inserted the spike. Then I gave M6 the crate number I remembered.

I fired a few blind shots toward likely hiding spots. The bay doors started to close again.

"M6, we need to move—now!"

"Still working. Security protocols are...customized."

"Perfect."

The loader legs twitched, then began to move toward the door—but it was already sealed.

Next plan.

Across the bay, I spotted a yellow cylinder marked with a hazard symbol.

"What's in that tank?" I asked.

"Chlorine gas."

I fired two shots. Greenish-yellow vapor hissed out. Alarms blared.

Doors reopened.

I hobbled forward, then another shot hit me from behind. Likely the tower attacker, back in the fray.

I ducked behind the walking loader's legs, scanning with my gravimetric sensor.

Nothing—until something slammed into me from the side.

I went down.

A figure straddled me—Ghost armor—and fired point-blank into my visor.

I watched it begin to crack.

Chapter: Twenty-Nine

This had been a desperate move on the part of my attackers, but it had paid off. I was vulnerable—but not out of the fight. I could see the white-outlined image of the person on top of me now.

Instinct took over. My hands shot into action, grabbing for the arm with the gun. I think I gripped the wrist and pushed the barrel just far enough away that I was no longer taking shots to the head.

My assailant countered by delivering a fist to my face instead. This gave me an opportunity to trap the other arm and pull the person down, right into a headbutt. I made sure to impact with the upper part of my helmet so as not to further damage the already glitching HUD display. Then I followed up with my left hand, delivering a couple of elbow strikes to the head. Still gripping the right wrist, I used it for my coup de grâce.

With some wiggle room and my attacker's disorientation, I slid my left leg out and wrapped it across the chest, pushing the operative to the floor as I hyperextended the elbow—until I felt something give way.

I knew I'd broken the bone, but because of the attackers phasing, I heard no scream or crack from them. Now on my knees and scrambling for cover back under the legs of the load lifter droid, I took several hits to the back.

The other assailant was close by. Once on my feet and moving with the rhythm of the lifter's legs, I scanned the bay, firing at slight movement before it vanished behind one of the bipedal loaders.

"Since you only have some of the crate numbers," M6 said, "I was able to identify several possible locations. The one with the highest probability is a construction site near the embassy."

"Makes sense," I replied. "What's my fastest route there?"

"Since we are unsure of Ethan's timeline—or your vision—I suggest we steal another vehicle and head there immediately."

"Is the Chancellor on the planet?" I asked.

"Yes, and almost at the embassy, according to police chatter," M6 confirmed.

I was now outside the Hub, still shadowing the lifter. I could see flashing lights in the distance. Emergency crews were on their way. My mysterious third attacker had vanished—no longer pursuing me.

I glanced back into the Hub, hoping to catch movement, but saw none. In my mind, the operative was extracting their team. It's what I would've done.

Which raised the question: had my attackers been a CEF Ghost Recon team?

"I've spotted a vehicle nearby," M6 said. "It's another older model—should be no problem to hack."

At this rate, I was quickly becoming a world-class criminal. "Next time we have to steal something, let me pick it out," I muttered. "I'd like something a little flashier than this bland two-door you picked."

"Noted," M6 replied as I dropped into the seat.

***

What started as a calm little drive through the skylanes of Athens quickly became a death-defying test of skill.

I'd pulled away from the Hub with no pursuit. Halfway to my destination, however, two police vehicles—painted in the standard black, red, and orange—appeared behind me and lit up their sirens.

I had no choice now. I had to run. I wondered how this had happened. M6 confirmed everything about the vehicle was legal, but two explanations came to mind: either one of the operatives had spotted me and reported the theft—or the owner realized their car was missing and called it in.

Either way, I had to deal with it.

The fastest way to shake the police was to dive into the oncoming skylane traffic. Risky. Possibly fatal. But necessary.

"This is not a good idea," M6 warned.

"Too late," I replied, as my vehicle scraped along the side of a transport vehicle with a long screech. Another oncoming car forced me to swerve hard, barely avoiding impact.

In the rearview mirror, I saw the police hadn't followed. Instead, they accelerated and mirrored my movement from the adjacent lane.

Time to change that.

I aimed at the next oncoming vehicle, hoping to push it into their lane and cause enough chaos to end the pursuit.

Instead, I was clipped and slammed back into the original skylane—crashing into one of the police vehicles. It was damaged, but both cruisers fell back, now keeping their distance.

They were trying to avoid escalation. I didn't want to hurt anyone either. But if I didn't find the nukes, we were all dead. That much I knew.

"You're almost at the location," M6 reported.

Ahead, I saw the skeletal frame of the under-construction building piercing the sky. Beside it, smaller and circular, was the embassy—overgrown with green vines.

I saw no reason to lose the cops. If I found the nuke, I might even turn them to my side.

I dove for the building's upper floors and made a skidding landing, slamming into a support pillar. The police didn't follow inside. I saw them circling outside the level instead.

Time was running out.

I found a worker elevator and rode it down. I'd seen lifter droids on my approach.

"Searching through the records," M6 said. "The crate was delivered here a few days ago—about the same time work was paused due to the Artran Chancellor's arrival."

"Good to know. Let's find it."

***

A few minutes later, I found the crate sitting in the middle of the lobby. A few others surrounded it, but none had the same numbers.

I approached cautiously and had M6 scan it thoroughly before touching the control pad.

It took only a simple command. The crate split open on all four sides.

It was empty.

"M6, are you detecting any radiation residue?" I asked.

"None," came the reply.

Had I been tricked again? Was Ethan really that much smarter than me?

I didn't have time to stew in self-doubt. A familiar voice called my name from behind.

"Jericho," I said, turning to see the short-haired woman staring at me, her helmet off.

She'd been at the Hub. Those other operatives must have been her team. That explained how they'd countered every move I made.

"We need to talk, Jack," Jericho said.

She wasn't armed. Her posture wasn't threatening. Still, I did a quick gravimetric scan before coming out of phase.

Now eye to eye with her, I heard gunshots ring out from the embassy across the street.

It was happening—whatever Ethan had planned was unfolding.

The only question now was…
Was Jericho part of that plan?

Chapter: Thirty

If Jericho heard the gunshots, she made no reaction to them. Looking past her at the police standing just outside the embassy doors, it was obvious they weren't reacting either.

Then there was more shooting—still no response.

"Do you hear the gunfight going on at the embassy?" I asked.

Her gaze never left mine. "No," she said, stepping closer.

"Jack, I appreciate your efforts in not killing my team back at the Hub, but this little one-man war you've got going has to come to an end."

Why wasn't she hearing the firefight? It was obvious now.

"Ethan is here on Mars," I said, "and he intends to reignite the war with the Artrans."

Jericho shook her head, taking two more steps toward me. "Ethan is dead, Jack. A recovery team found biological remains of Ethan and the executives—attached to fragments of the *Elminster*. There is no threat."

"But he came to me in New York, tricked me into believing he was Thadd, and set this whole thing in motion. He's playing a game with me."

"Do you hear yourself?" Jericho asked. "Jack, look at me. I would never lie to you. You're having a mental breakdown. Let me help you get better. It's what Beverly wants too."

"I can't do that, Jericho. If I don't stop Ethan, millions will die. If not from the nukes he took from Septis Four, then from the war he'll start again. I can't allow that."

Her gaze dropped slightly as she shook her head again. "And I can't allow you to keep going. Too many people have already been hurt by your actions."

"As you know, there is no perfect operation without risk—to yourself, your team, or the public," I said.

"The same words you gave me on our first assignment together," Jericho said. "Please, Jack. Let's not end things this way."

"What way is that, Jericho?" I asked, slowly moving my hand toward my pistol. I didn't want to kill her—but how much time did I have left before Ethan detonated the nuke?

"I guess today I'll find out if I've surpassed the master," she said, a small grin spreading across her lips.

She rushed me.

She was quick, closing the distance and delivering a devastating blow toward my visor with the butt end of a blade I hadn't even seen her draw. I had the pistol out of the holster, but before I could fire, she knocked it from my hand with a well-timed kick.

Kicks were naturally slower to execute, giving me just enough time to back away and begin unlocking the helmet from the chest plate. Jericho could've taken the opportunity to strike a killing blow, but she was showing restraint—stretching out the fight.

I knew how this woman thought. Just as she knew how I did.

With the helmet off and tossed to the floor, she spoke again.

"Now we're face-to-face, Jack. Look me in the eye and listen to me. End this now."

"I can't," I said. "There's too much at stake. If you'll just trust me, Jericho... I'm not having a mental breakdown. Walk with me across the street—let's see what's happening."

She glanced toward the embassy, then back at me—before launching another attack.

This time, I was better prepared. I saw the blade coming. She wasn't holding back—short stabbing strikes aimed at my face, trying to get in close to strike a joint.

My hands moved in short, practiced slaps to deflect the blade. One strike nicked the side of my cheek. She pressed in close, using my flinch to her advantage.

I knew what was coming—my instincts kicking in. I swept a palm near my waist and twisted hard to the right. The tip of the blade hit my armor instead of soft tissue.

My other hand struck her face, connecting with her nose and drawing blood.

She paused—just long enough for me to grab her with both hands and deliver a series of vicious knees toward her stomach. She blocked with both hands, but not before I landed one or two.

She grunted from the pain. Then, with incredible skill, she timed my next knee perfectly—grabbing my thigh with one hand, my arm with the other, and pulled me into a vicious headbutt that shattered my nose. I felt the blood pour and tasted copper in the back of my throat.

My vision blurred. My body recoiled from the hit, instinct overriding all else.

If it hadn't been for M6's warning—*duck and roll*—I would be dead.

Rolling to my feet, I detached the blade from its recessed position on the back of my right thigh plate. Jericho was already on me, stabbing again.

Disoriented, my reactions lagged. She got in close. This time, I pivoted hard, without using my hands to block. Her blade slipped into the gap at my leg joint.

Pain tore through my body, but I forced myself to finish the move. My blade found its target—a vulnerable point along her side—and drove deep.

Much deeper than I'd intended.

She stumbled back, staring down at the blade still stuck in her side.

Wiping my eyes, I saw crimson pour from the wound.

She looked up at me, then collapsed to her knees.

The blade she had used clattered to the floor. I saw her fumbling for a medkit in her utility cylinder.

I rushed to her side, kneeling, reaching for my own kit. But then she fell back, one hand going limp while the other stretched toward me.

I had bandages in hand, but I didn't know what to do. I couldn't remove the blade without killing her. From the amount of blood... I'd likely hit an artery.

With trembling fingers, she gripped my hand. Tears streaked her pale cheeks.

"I hope you were right," she whispered—and closed her eyes.

"Jericho," I said, still holding her hand. "Why did this happen? Why couldn't you see the truth? Jericho...don't go."

I let go of her hand and began chest compressions.

"Jack," M6 said gently. "She's gone. There's nothing more you can do."

"No! Dammit, Jericho, you're tougher than this!"

"It's over," M6 said. "But you can still save the others."

I stopped. Sat there on my knees, aching, bruised, bleeding.

It should've been me lying there. Jericho was younger, faster, well-trained. Why was I still alive?

"The gunfire at the embassy has gone silent," M6 reported. "With no new clues on the location of the nuclear devices, our next course of action is to find Ethan and stop him."

There was no arguing with that logic. Everything pointed to the embassy. Ethan had to be there.

I touched Jericho's face and whispered, "I'm sorry."

Then I got to my feet, retrieved my weapons, and placed Jericho's helmet on my head.

It smelled faintly of her shampoo—fruity and bright. I forced the thought from my mind as I re-engaged the phase.

It was time to end this—one way or another.

Chapter: Thirty-One

The police were still standing around by the embassy door, talking casually about upcoming sports. The vehicles that had pursued me here were still circling in the sky, but so far, no one had entered.

Everything felt wrong—strange, almost like a dream.

I walked through the embassy doors and found people sitting at the counter, smiling and calmly making small talk with coworkers. I stepped into the lift, half-expecting some reaction from them—as if an invisible force had just summoned it—but they just kept chatting.

"Forty-ninth floor," M6 said.

"That's at the top," I replied, pressing the button.

"I was able to triangulate the acoustics of the gunshots. This was the level they came from."

I checked over my rifle to ensure nothing was damaged, bringing it to rest across my chest. Jericho's death still weighed heavily on my mind. Despite several deep breaths, I couldn't get her face out of my head.

When the doors opened, a middle-aged man in business attire slumped halfway into the lift. Only the upper half of his body remained—multiple gunshot wounds had clearly ended his life.

The hallway beyond was darkened. Most of the lights had been shot out, and the remaining few flickered in an almost hypnotic rhythm.

As I moved forward, I spotted more bodies up ahead. More well-dressed victims, obviously representatives from the Colonial Earth Systems. They had come to witness a historic signing. Instead, they now lay face down on the thick gray carpeting, most of them shot in the back as they fled.

It wasn't until I reached the ornate wooden doors that I discovered the source of the violence.

Several security police had turned on the unarmed Artrans, who now lay dead around the circular chamber. From the look of it, the Artrans had rushed the guards in a desperate attempt to stop the massacre.

Oddly, it also appeared that some embassy staff had joined in the violence, using bare hands or even chairs to assault the Artrans. Those who tried to flee were shot down by the guards.

"None of this scene makes sense," M6 said.

"Agreed. Have you found the Chancellor yet?"

Before M6 could respond, a loud metallic clank rang out—a heavy door slamming shut nearby.

I immediately moved toward the sound. Was it possible there were survivors? Or had Ethan returned to examine his handiwork?

From my encounter in Novick City, I had a sense of Ethan's telepathic abilities—but after what happened here, it was clear he had grown more powerful.

The door I'd heard closing was a thick fire escape exit in the hallway. I pulled it open cautiously and peered in, just in time to hear another door slam shut from above.

I was already on the top floor. That meant whoever fled was now on the rooftop.

"Is there a way off the roof?" I asked.

"Unknown," M6 replied.

Taking the stairs two at a time, I reached the final door and pushed through, only to find myself in a bay filled with small shuttles.

One of the shuttles was already lifting off, heading straight for the domed ceiling. I noticed something strange—lights on the dome strobed red at first, then turned green. A transparent section slid open, allowing the shuttle to pass through before sealing shut again.

A private port—built specifically for embassy use.

I spotted another shuttle nearby with its ramp down and took off running. Once inside, it became clear the area had been abandoned. It should've been buzzing with maintenance crews and security, but it was eerily quiet.

Everything in the shuttle was powered on when I sat down, suggesting people had fled mid-task.

"Well, that was too easy," I muttered, strapping into the pilot's seat. The consoles and interfaces were standard Earth design.

"Do you have a trajectory for that shuttle?" I asked.

"Not yet," M6 replied.

"How about opening that port in the dome?"

"I've already sent the command."

I didn't waste time responding. Instead, I launched straight up at breakneck speed, needing to catch up with the escaping vessel.

Through the first portal, I had to pause as the lower section sealed behind me and the upper dome retracted. When it opened wide enough, I blasted upward again, pushing the inertial dampers to their limit.

"The shuttle is heading toward the Artran warship just outside orbit," M6 said.

Had the Chancellor survived? How was that possible?

"I've also found the *Kuroseki*," M6 added. "It's on an intercept course."

"Hail them," I said.

"No need. They're hailing us."

I leaned back. "Put it on."

The image of Ethan appeared, standing before a large transparasteel window, gazing down at Mars.

"I have to say, Jack, I'm really impressed with your survivability and tenacity. Was it the death of your family that made you this way?"

"Stop this, Ethan. You've already done what you wanted. The CEF and Artrans will continue the war after today. There's no stopping that now."

"True," Ethan said. "But I'm not done yet. You still doubt their telepathic abilities. I have the proof now. I've much to show you. Please—come aboard."

It was an open invitation. And if Ethan was talking, he wasn't pressing buttons that could kill millions.

"I look forward to it," I said, adjusting course to dock with the *Kuroseki*.

***

I was greeted with smiles from unarmed officers as they escorted me through the corporate vessel to the observation room where Ethan waited.

He stood before the window, hands clasped behind his back, staring down at Mars. The two officers left without a word, and I was left alone with him.

There were no guards. No restraints. I still had my weapons.

It would be easy to end this.

Ethan glanced over his shoulder. "I know what you're thinking, Jack. You want to put a bullet in my skull. Go ahead—try it."

Without hesitation, I raised my rifle and fired.

Every shot missed him, striking the parasteel window behind.

What the hell?

"I fear nothing, Jack," Ethan said. "I see everything now. Humans are the inheritors of this galaxy—now that the Nah-aloy are gone."

"Nah-aloy?" I asked, stepping closer.

Ethan turned to face me. "Sorry—you know them as the Ancients."

"Where did you get this information? And how do you know it's valid?"

That smug, all-knowing grin returned. "I've touched the mind of one of them, Jack. Not all are dead. Thousands lie in stasis, waiting for a cure to the wasting virus that nearly wiped them out."

A good piece of fiction. But no way to prove it.

"I know you're not easily persuaded. So I'll answer the question you haven't asked: the omega mirror. We thought it was broken—beyond repair. But Omicron got it working again. And it's mine now. Look around. Notice anything familiar?"

I looked. Plush chairs. Marble statues. And there, near the wall—the familiar metallic oval of the omega mirror.

If what he said was true…if the mirror worked… Ethan's powers could be on a whole new level. The stuff of legend—able to influence entire worlds.

Ethan turned back to the window. "I've touched the minds of gods, Jack. The CEF has no idea what dangers await in the dark. But I can lead them. Quietly. I don't want control—I want influence. Like the wizard behind the curtain."

Was that a *Wizard of Oz* reference? Jennifer had hated that movie. The flying monkeys scared her.

"I hear a lot of big talk, Ethan. Where's this proof you keep bragging about?"

"Right here," he said, pressing a button on a console.

A holographic projection lit up, showing a panoramic view of the embassy just before the massacre. The Artran Chancellor stood at center stage, surrounded by warriors.

He looked frail—thinner than the others. When he spoke, his voice came in clicking and whistling tones. No translation played, but it triggered a violent reaction from several attendees.

People began throwing items—pens, notebooks, even chairs. Human security moved in, trying to calm the chaos, but more joined in the violence.

"This is you?" I asked, pointing to the crowd.

Ethan nodded. "Watch what happens next."

At first, it seemed Ethan had incited everyone against the Artrans. But then, chaos turned inward. Some humans started attacking each other.

"That part wasn't me," Ethan said. "The Chancellor is a telepath. Stronger than me."

I turned toward him. His hands were now crossed over his chest.

"Why are you certain it's the Chancellor?" I asked.

"Because, Jack, you're about to see something I've only glimpsed once. And that was enough to scare the hell out of me."

I kept watching.

As the fighting escalated, bodies piled up. Several of the Chancellor's honor guard fell—but then something horrifying happened.

They stood back up.

Limp, lifeless, marionette-like.

Human and Artran corpses—walking again.

It could have been unconsciousness. But no…I saw two Artran warriors with crushed skulls get back up.

What in the hell was I witnessing?

"This is some kind of necromancer bullshit," I muttered.

"That's why I target the brain stem," Ethan said. "It's the only way to keep them down."

"You saw this in a vision?"

"Yes. While in prison. As I was regaining my abilities."

I stared at the projection. "This is terrifying. The Council will want to examine this thoroughly."

Ethan looked down at the console. His voice dropped.

"That's why I'm not giving them a choice."

He pressed a button.

A bright white flash burst through the observation window.

I staggered forward in horror.

He had done it.

Ethan had detonated the nuke in the Athens colony.

Millions—gone in an instant.

All because Ethan wanted the war to continue.

And I had been a fool to believe I could stop him with words.

Chapter: Thirty-Two

Anger filled me, and like a raging river, I charged Ethan, intent on causing serious harm. Except the man moved with extraordinary skill and precision.

He sidestepped my charge just enough for me to plow into the wooden table, smashing part of it to the floor with splintering cracks.

"Go ahead, Jack. Get all that anger out of you. You'll feel better," Ethan said.

His voice only enraged me further. I swung at his face with all I had, but he caught my fist in a familiar hand drill I'd practiced countless times myself. Before I could counter, his fist smashed into my nose, and blood poured—he followed it up with an elbow strike to the jaw.

When I hit the floor, I was sure my jaw was broken. But it still moved under my command. Blood was streaming freely down my face.

Normally, I would've sprung back to my feet and pressed the attack. But Ethan was already ahead of me, delivering a kick to my ribs that left me rolling onto my back, unable to breathe, much less move.

"Jack," Ethan said calmly, "I'll be honest with you. Under normal circumstances, you're the better fighter. I wouldn't fare well in this exchange. But you didn't learn your lesson from the gunfire earlier. You *can't* hurt me."

I heard his words, but all I could think about was the overwhelming pain. I turned to my uninjured side, trying to breathe, blood pooling around my head.

When I could finally speak again, I whispered to M6, "Any suggestions?"

"None," M6 replied.

I didn't respond. Instead, I crawled toward the observation window and propped myself up against it, staring down at the still-mushrooming cloud.

"What I've set in motion," Ethan said, moving closer, "cannot be undone. The war will continue—and we *will* bring an end to the Artran."

I couldn't even argue. I scooted away from the window and sat on my knees in a shiza position. Meditation was the only way to clear my mind. Right now, I had no direction—everything was chaos.

My nose was busted, so I had to inhale and exhale slowly through my aching mouth. I visualized all the pain as a balloon swelling up, then released it into the wind.

Within seconds, the technique worked—just as it always had. The pain dulled.

Ethan's breath brushed my face as he knelt beside me. "You and your ancient meditation practices. I never understood them, Jack."

I let the words enter and drift away on an invisible breeze. Despite the carnage and confusion, I had found a few moments of clarity.

That's when I saw it.

For the first time, I realized why I hadn't been able to hurt Ethan. The Ethan kneeling beside me was an *illusion*, implanted in my mind.

By quieting my thoughts, I now saw the *real* Ethan—seated at the broken table, watching me.

My hand went for my pistol, strapped to my thigh. With one smooth motion, I twisted my body and fired a shot square into Ethan's chest.

A red stain blossomed from the wound. Ethan looked down at it, stunned.

I got to my feet and moved toward the omega mirror.

There wasn't much thought behind what I did next—just instinct. For some reason, I believed I could use the omega mirror to stop the war before it began again.

"Jack," Ethan stammered, breathing shallowly, "don't give into it... It will kill you..."

My own death didn't matter anymore. I had no family left. I'd killed one of my own teammates. None of it mattered—except ending this war.

As I stepped closer, the mirror's silvery surface rippled, reflecting my image—as if it knew I was present.

"Let's do this," I said, locking eyes with my reflection. I could *feel* the presence of something watching—not one entity, but many.

I was like a lab rat under a microscope.

"I want to end this war," I shouted in my mind, not knowing if the observers could hear me.

The world around me faded to black. Then streaks of light flashed across my vision—faster and faster—until I stood upon a white sand plain under a white sun.

Dunes rose in the distance. On the horizon stood humanoid figures—black silhouettes—silent and unmoving. I couldn't make out their features, but I could hear their voices inside my mind—not as one, but as many:

"What you ask is possible," they said. "To do so will kill you."

"I'm willing," I said.

"Such a noble act," they replied. "Perhaps...they will be worthy one day."

"Worthy of what?" I asked.

But before I could get an answer, the white sun exploded in a blinding flash, and everything was ripped away into darkness.

***

My eyes fluttered open.

I was back on the floor, staring at my wife. She knelt nearby, her arm extended toward me.

She was beckoning me to come to her.

"Jack," M6 said, his voice urgent. "You are experiencing massive brain trauma. You need surgical attention immediately."

I could barely move, but I inched closer to her.

I just wanted to feel her embrace again—to feel her warmth, her love, one more time.

"You must remain motionless," M6 said.

"I can't," I whispered, inching forward.

If I could just stretch out my hand far enough…

"Jack," M6 warned, "I must remind you—what you're seeing is not real. You are dying."

"Goodbye, M6," I said softly, as my hand finally reached hers.

This felt right.

I was home at last.

Chapter: Thirty-Three

INTERLUDE: ADMIRAL THADD

Location: Earth, **Elysium Grounds** – *Cumberland Plateau, Tennessee*
Clearance Level: OMEGA-CLASSIFIED
Timestamp: 08:00 Galactic Standard

Thadd rubbed his eyes as his driver flew him over the countryside. Rain poured heavily outside the windows, and he could hear the patter of droplets striking the vehicle.

There was no music playing. He had planned to nap during the journey, but he couldn't help glancing out at the undamaged land below.

Sometimes he wished he were just one of the common folk—waking up to watch the news, eat breakfast, and head off to a regular day job. When he was younger, he'd liked working with his hands. There was something deeply satisfying about building something from scratch—a true sense of accomplishment that a desk job simply couldn't provide.

Maybe he would've taken a job as a mechanic back in his teens. Instead, he had enlisted in the Colonial Earth Forces before the war. The allure of seeing other worlds and alien life had appealed to him then.

Now, he was burdened with the affairs of not just Earth, but its colonies as well. Mars was still reeling from the loss of its major city and hub. And if that wasn't enough, there were growing problems in the Delta Quadrant of space.

"Sir," the young driver called from the front, "we've arrived at the gravesite."

Thadd rubbed his eyes again and searched for his coffee in the center console. Its warmth had long since faded. He wasn't due for a meeting until 1300 hours; it was only 0800. That gave him time— time to try and explain things to Beverly.

After everything that had happened, he owed her that. He hoped it might help sway her into returning to duty. After all, it had been a couple of months since the incident on Mars. And she had delivered her baby without any complications. He needed every seasoned officer he could get right now.

"Do you want me to carry the umbrella, sir?" the driver asked.

Thadd just shook his head and opened the door. Unfolding a large, oversized black umbrella, he stepped out. His feet squished into the soaked grass as he approached the headstone.

Beverly was already there, glancing back as he neared. When he stood beside her, she offered a salute.

"Thanks for coming," she said, lowering her hand and looking back at the headstone.

They stood in front of Jack's and Elizabeth's grave. The ground on Jack's side had been freshly dug, with a date newly carved into the stone.

"I need to know," she said quietly.

"I was going to brief you on the details," Thadd replied. "There's been a lot happening since the Mars incident—and that telepathic blast everyone received. It terrified people from the top down."

"Was it Jack who sent it?" she asked.

A cool breeze brushed his face, and he took a quick breath before answering. "We think so. Jack's body, along with Ethan's, was never recovered. We know they were both aboard the corporate vessel *Kuroseki*. We have plenty of video evidence and eyewitness reports. But no one knows how they got off the ship. We found a lot of Ethan's blood in one location—he was bleeding heavily. Jack was injured too; we found his blood in several places."

"Then Jack could be alive?" she asked. "Why the rush to bury him, then?"

"It's been over two months, Beverly. The CEF wanted to close the case quickly—our resources were needed elsewhere."

"Sounds about right," she muttered, shooting him a sidelong look. "Jack was a hero to the very end. That telepathic message warned everyone about the Artran threat. And it was Ethan who set off the nuke. Jack tried to warn us, Admiral—but we didn't listen. If we had, maybe Mars wouldn't be bleeding right now."

Thadd stood there silently, letting the rain wash over him as he gathered his thoughts. What he said next could determine whether Beverly came back or not.

"I know," he said finally. "I regret that decision every day, Beverly. But that's in the past now. All we can do is try to shape the future. That's what Jack would've wanted. That's what Jericho would've wanted."

"Don't bring her into this," Beverly snapped. "I've seen the video of their fight. She left Jack with little choice."

"I agree," Thadd said. "Beverly, what I'm about to say isn't what you want to hear, but I have to say it anyway. I need you back in service. The fallout from the telepathic blast, Mars, and now the situation in the Delta Quadrant…the galaxy is anything but at peace."

"I don't know," she said, shaking her head and looking down at the headstone again. "He should've had a proper CEF funeral. Jack was a hero. He should be remembered and celebrated."

"It will happen," Thadd assured her. "It'll just take time. Let the wounds heal, and then the truth can come out. Jack will be celebrated as the hero he was, Beverly. I promise you that."

She didn't look at him, but he could tell she was crying, dabbing her nose with a tissue.

"If I come back," she said, "I want access to any and all information we have on Jack, Ethan, and every possible lead about where they might have gone."

This was promising.

"I swear to you—it'll be done."

Her eyes met his, steady and measuring, unblinking. Then she broke eye contact.

"I'll report back in forty-eight hours."

Without another word, she turned and walked away.

Thadd looked down at Jack's headstone one last time. A few words slipped out.

"I wish I could've done more, Jack. I'm sorry for that. Goodbye, old friend."

It felt like some closure, he thought, walking back to the vehicle. The driver opened the door, and moments later, they were airborne once more.

Part: III

Chapter: Thirty-Four

I opened my eyes to a white light. This was it—the tunnel so often described by those who'd had near-death experiences. I was dead. But why did my skin feel so cold? And what were those beeping noises in the background?

Blinking a few times, the bright light vanished, replaced by a man in a white hood and mask looking down at me.

I wasn't dead. How was that possible? I'd seen Elizabeth reaching out to me. I *knew* she was pulling me into the afterlife. It had to be real.

"Don't try to move," a male voice said. "You've been in a coma for months."

A coma? I tried to lift my arms, finding they responded slowly to my commands.

"I told you not to move," the voice repeated.

To hell with this person. I *should* be dead—I *knew* I was dead. Forcing my arms into motion, I managed to sit up in the hospital bed.

Everything was blurry at first, but as my eyes adjusted to the fluorescent lighting, I took in my surroundings. It was definitely a medical clinic of some kind—new, sterile, and well-maintained.

Oddly, I felt like I was underground.

"Where am I?" I asked, eyeing the technician in the white plastic suit and hood. The room was large, but empty—no other patients or staff.

The man replied, "Director Lorna is on her way down to see you. She'll explain everything."

Director? Was I in a Greystone Corporation medical facility? I'd been aboard one of their corporate ships. Was this still a ship?

The feeling of being underground wouldn't leave me. Maybe it was the damp chill in the air—or the claustrophobic, rounded tunnel I glimpsed outside the door.

I sat for a few minutes on the edge of the bed, wiggling my toes and pondering everything. That's when two women in pure white dresses entered the room.

The one in the lead had raven hair pulled into a tight ponytail and wore bright red lipstick. She was slightly taller than the brunette walking behind her.

"Jackson Howard Donovan," the dark-haired woman said. "My name is Director Lorna. I'm sure you have many questions—but first, let me congratulate you on becoming part of our family."

What the hell does that mean?

"Family?"

Lorna smiled, revealing perfect white teeth. "You now belong to the Zytec Corporation."

It took me a few seconds to pull fragments of memory together. If I still had my neural link with M6, it would've already been feeding me data. *I wonder if he's nearby.*

What I *did* remember was that Zytec was the second company to expand into space. They had established their own colony dedicated to research. Their headquarters were on Earth, of course—

but out here, on the fringe of human-controlled space, who knew what they'd been doing?

"I see a flicker of recognition," Lorna said. "As a member of our family, Jack, you're entitled to some of our most exclusive patented therapies. How old would you guess I am?"

Was this a recruiting speech?

"Don't care," I muttered, planting my feet on the cold floor. My body started to shiver almost immediately.

"There's no need to be rude, Jack. Zytec owns you, after all," Lorna said.

I felt unsteady at first. The technician tried to help me stand, but I waved him off. I didn't need his damn help. What I *needed* was to get the hell out of here.

"Still don't care," I said, pushing past the director. The brunette behind her gave me pause. My eyes locked on hers instantly—brown, familiar, intense.

She looked so much like Elizabeth—except her nose was thinner, her cheekbones higher. And for some reason, I *wanted* this woman. I was already imagining our bodies locked in a passionate embrace.

Was she a telepath?

She reached a hand toward me, and I instinctively stepped back.

"Interesting," Lorna said.

"Are you a telepath?" I asked, finding myself suddenly pinned back against the bed by the presence of the two women. I couldn't tear my gaze away from the brunette.

"Sophia, leave us," Lorna said. "I think you're making our new guest a little too excited."

Sophia left the room, and I couldn't help but watch her go.

"To answer your question," Lorna said, "no, she's not a telepath. She produces a unique pheromone—her body's own creation."

I kept staring at the door, hoping she'd return.

"She also happens to be the one who rescued you from the *Kuroseki*. You were fortunate one of our agents was nearby—otherwise, you'd be dead."

A flashback hit me. I was lying on the ground, reaching toward my wife—but on reflection, it wasn't Elizabeth I saw. It was Sophia. Her lips were moving. She was speaking to me. But I couldn't make out the words.

The last image was of her cradling me and injecting something into my neck.

"You should've let me die," I said, my heart rate spiking. "I was ready."

Lorna's dark blue eyes locked onto mine. "I realize that, Jack—especially after everything you've been through. The death of your wife and child. The innocents lost on your path to stop Ethan."

She reached out and gently touched my face. Her hand was soft, almost too soft.

"You're right—I should've let you die. But that telepathic blast of images you sent out...it touched every mind in the galaxy. After that, we had no choice. We had to acquire you."

"You keep talking like I'm property."

Lorna dropped her hand. "You're not *my* property, technically. But you *are* property—of Zytec Corporation. Your face and DNA have been altered. The only thing that's still you, Jack, is your brain. That powerful, extraordinary brain."

I looked around, scanning for anything reflective. There—a tall mirror on the wall behind me. I twisted my head and caught a glimpse of a stranger.

What in the hell had they done to me?

I had thick brown hair, mussed from the pillow. My eyes were no longer blue, but deep jade. My skin and features looked like I was in my twenties again.

"Remarkable, isn't it?" Lorna said.

I shoved past her and stepped into the hallway. Other doors lined the corridor. I tried each handle—they were all locked, refusing to budge even as I threw my weight against them.

The hallway curved left, but I chose to go right. It ended in another corridor that branched left and right. I kept going left, testing doors as I passed.

Then I saw her—Sophia—opening a door at the end.

I sprinted toward her.

But instead of stepping aside, she moved *into* my path, wrapping her arms and legs around me as we tumbled into the room behind her.

Our lips met instantly, tongues battling for control. I felt the heat of her body, the beat of her heart beneath her skin. It was hard to resist. And for a moment—I didn't.

Then I was on my back.

Paralyzed.

Sophia straightened her white dress, now smiling as she looked down at me.

"Perhaps we can continue this at a later time," she said, nodding as Lorna entered the room.

"Jack," Lorna said, "I knew you'd be a handful when we took you in. But in time, you'll learn to obey."

The hell I will, I thought, straining to will my body to move.

Chapter: Thirty-Five

A couple of men in white technician suits entered the room, lifted me up off the floor and sat me down in a metal chair. I couldn't move my head—I was permanently locked staring down at my feet as Lorna spoke.

"Now that I have your complete attention, Jack, we can continue our discussion from earlier. As stated, you are now the property of Zytec Corporation."

I saw her black high-heeled shoes just inches from my own.

"Your brain is still recovering from massive trauma. Many of our doctors believe you'll never be telepathic again. But that doesn't mean we can't use your other skills. In fact, we're in desperate need of a man like you, Jack."

She moved behind me, and I felt her hands gripping near my neck.

"Zytec has a lot of enemies—especially out here on the fringe of CEF-controlled space. I'm sure you're aware of the Voidborn pirates that operate out of the Golar Nebula?"

I knew about them. But I still couldn't respond. The pirates had never been my problem—unless they'd stumbled into one of my ops. When they first emerged, the CEF actually welcomed their attacks on the Artrans. But as the war dragged on, desperation took hold. They started hitting CEF supply ships too.

"The Voidborn took something from us recently, and we want it back—no matter the cost. That's where you come in. With your skills and the right tools, you're the perfect candidate to infiltrate their group and recover what was stolen."

She began massaging the muscles around my neck. I felt a tingling sensation from the pressure.

"The good news," Lorna said, "is that we recovered your armor. Our technicians restored it—better than new, actually. Much better than that Omicron Technologies junk. You know, Zytec had the original contract for the Ghost Recon armor—until we were underbid."

I could feel my fingers twitch. At last, I could form words with my drooling lips.

"What about M6?"

"Don't worry. Your AI companion is still safely loaded in the armor. We waited to wake you so we could ask—do you want him installed into a new DIM-series body?"

"I want to talk to him," I said, raising my head slowly.

"And you will, soon. But first, there are a few little things I need to inform you of—just in case you're thinking about using this mission to escape. First, your body now requires an injection every couple of days. Miss a dose, and you'll grow weak—eventually incapacitated."

She leaned closer. "Second, we have ways of tracking you that you can't even imagine. If you run, a retrieval team will be dispatched to drag your ass back. Don't make us use that option. Failure is punished, Jack—and there are more ways to torture someone than just physically."

I could move my arms now. I wasn't strong enough to stand, but rage was building inside me. They really believed they could own me—control me. I could rain destruction on this place so fast they'd never recover.

Lorna withdrew her hands from my shoulders.

"Move Jack to his quarters," she ordered the technicians, "before he gets too bold."

I couldn't resist. My arms were too weak, and I couldn't push the men away. I screamed as they dragged me from the room.

For the first time, I saw where I'd been. It looked like an armory. Rifles, pistols, and body armor lined the walls. Many racks were empty—perhaps losses from the pirate raid she'd mentioned.

If I could just get back in there again...

"We'll continue this discussion later, Jack," Lorna called after me. "Take this time to think over everything I've told you."

Minutes later, I was lying on a small single-person bed, white sheets beneath me, white ceiling above, white lights glaring down.

I could finally move all my extremities, but I didn't get up. I stayed there, Lorna's words echoing in my mind.

I wasn't going to be a tool. I wasn't a pawn. I was a *free man*—and I would choose my own destiny. Even if that destiny led me back to death.

I had welcomed it, back on that ship. I'd been ready. I just wanted to see my family again.

Closing my eyes, a memory surged forward.

The coffins. Lowered into frozen earth at a snow-covered gravesite.

I covered my face as tears streamed down. They had tried to keep me from seeing the bodies before burial—but I had looked anyway.

Jenifer's once-perfect ivory skin was blue and black, and part of her face had been crushed by debris. My wife, on the other hand, was just… blue. The report read like a horror novel. It was possible she'd survived for days—*conscious*—after Jenifer passed.

I couldn't imagine the terror she must've endured. In that bomb shelter with hundreds of other people, either being crushed to death by the debris collapsing down on them from an almost direct hit. Or the fact that a broken water main was filling the room with cold water.

I fell to my knees.

And right there, I made a vow:
I would not serve this corporation.
Starvation.
Disobedience.
Whatever it took.
Those would be my weapons.

Chapter: Thirty-six

It had been at least three days since I made my vow to starve. I'd kept track by the regular intervals at which a technician entered the room with a tempting plate of food.

At first, it was bland stuff—oatmeal, soup, or something equally forgettable. But as they realized I was serious about this endeavor, the meals became more enticing: sizzling bacon, juicy steaks, tender ribs. At one point, I was convinced they had redirected airflow from the kitchen into my tiny room.

Still, I remained cross-legged on the floor, focused on my breathing. Whenever images of the past—or temptation—entered my mind, I pushed them aside, always seeking the void between thoughts.

My body was screaming in protest, growing weaker with each passing hour. Standing had become a chore, and eventually, I collapsed into the bed, too exhausted to keep my eyes open.

The technicians had tried to intervene—hooking me up to IVs, applying life-saving measures—but I managed to fight them off. I wasn't sure what would happen next. Lorna likely wouldn't allow me to die.

Her most strategic move would be to wait until I was too weak to resist, then strap me to a gurney and pump fluids into my body. But even if that happened, this act was still one of defiance. I had resisted their control. I had shown them that if I died, I would do so *on my terms*. That had to mean something—to cost them something. Time, resources, and control.

Several hours had passed since the last untouched meal had been delivered. I figured another one was due soon. But the person who entered my room next wasn't a technician.

It was Sophia.

My eyes had been closed, but they flew open the moment she stepped inside. She wore a citrusy perfume today, and a short black dress that clung to her curves. Her lips were painted red—just like Lorna's—and a lacy black band circled her neck.

I should've expected Lorna to use this kind of temptation against me.

And the worst part?

It might work.

Sophia was stunning. And whatever her enhanced pheromones were doing to me, I could already feel my heart pounding in my chest. My breathing, once slow and controlled, had turned shallow and erratic.

She moved closer and knelt in front of me.

"When you started your starvation protest," she said, "I honestly didn't think you had the willpower to take it this far, Jack."

My lips and throat were so dry, they felt like sandpaper. Speaking was nearly impossible.

"Let me help you with that," she offered, retrieving a cup of water that had been left by the door. She dipped a finger into it and brought it to my lips.

Her touch sent a jolt through me—but I summoned what willpower I had left and pushed her hand away. Forcing the words out through cracked lips, I rasped, "Go away."

It was probably the last defiant act I could manage. I wanted that water more than anything. But I refused to give in.

She blinked in surprise, frozen for a moment. "You really are willing to go through with this."

I nodded.

"What if we were mated—you and me?" she asked softly. "Wouldn't that be worth living for? I could give you anything. Make any fantasy you've ever had come true. Imagine it, Jack. I'd do *anything* for you."

Visions of her—naked and warm—rushed into my mind. I pictured every pleasure she promised. I wanted her. My body screamed for her.

But I looked away.

Eyes shut tight, I focused on my breath. Slow. Measured.

"No," I whispered. "Out."

After a pause, she stood and left.

The temptation still lingered—but I had endured. I had passed another test.

Until the next visitor arrived.

This time, it wasn't a technician.

A man stepped into the room, gun in hand, and aimed it directly at my forehead.

Chapter: Thirty-Seven

The man with the gun was sweating and trembling as he spoke. "You…you killed them all. They didn't have to die."

My first instinct was to figure out what the hell he meant by that, but the more pressing concern was the trembling pistol aimed at my forehead.

Under normal circumstances, I'd have grabbed the barrel, shoved it aside, and lunged at him. But in my current state, that wasn't possible. And judging by the man's mental condition, reasoning wasn't going to work either.

So, once again, I found myself staring death in the face—and I wasn't going to blink.

From somewhere outside the room, I heard screams echoing in the hallway, followed by gunshots. The man in front of me turned toward the door, mumbling something incoherent, and—for reasons I couldn't begin to fathom—he walked out into the corridor and started firing.

More screams followed.

With great effort, I used the bed for support and forced myself to my feet.

Was this another pirate attack?

Nothing made sense. Two technicians ran past my door, each armed with a pistol. More gunfire erupted in the hallway.

"You'll never take me alive!" someone screamed.

Whatever was happening, it might just give me a chance to escape this place.

Stumbling toward the sink, I turned the cold water spigot on and let the freezing liquid touch my lips.
Bliss.

I didn't overdo it—just enough to soothe the dryness in my throat and lips. Then, staggering to the door, I slid it mostly shut, leaving a narrow gap to peer through.

From that angle, I couldn't see the full extent of the firefight, but I caught a glimpse of a body on the floor nearby—one of the technicians I'd seen rush past.

Thick crimson pooled beneath his head, and his arms were flung wide above him. His pistol had been thrown backward, away from the fighting.

I needed that gun.

Opening the door a little wider, I looked again. Several bodies now littered the hallway, and two men were locked in hand-to-hand combat near the lift.

Seizing the opportunity, I dropped to the ground and crawled like a child toward the weapon. Gripping it, I could feel the weight— it still had a nearly full clip.

No time to celebrate.

A technician emerged from another hallway, charging straight at me with a fire axe raised.

No time to think.

I pulled the trigger. The first two shots missed. The third and fourth hit him square in the chest. He crumpled forward, the axe clattering to the ground as his body fell almost on top of me.

A quick scan of the area revealed no immediate threats. The two men near the lift were now sprawled on the floor—either dead or unconscious. I didn't care which.

I had decisions to make.

First priority: get to that armory room.

I stood, pressing my back to the wall, and crept toward the end of the hallway. I peeked left, then right. No movement.

To my surprise, the armory door was wide open.

Was this really a pirate attack?
Or were these people turning on each other?

Whatever the case, it was chaos.

The armory was empty when I stepped inside. I scanned the room—there were pistols and rifles on the walls, but no clips, no ammo. Useless without supplies.

I had maybe fourteen bullets left. And no idea how many hostiles I'd face.

Then I spotted it.

A compact metal baton resting on a pedestal. It didn't look particularly useful, but something about it drew me in. It felt…alien.

The moment I touched it, my world changed.

***

I could see the weapon in my hand—small and compact. But the hand wasn't human. It was red-skinned and scaly, like an alligator's hide. The fingertips ended in thick talons.

Ahead, I saw a squad of Artran warriors moving through the corridor of a vessel.

Even though I was seeing through the creature's eyes, I wasn't in control—just a first-person observer. The alien gripped the baton, and it came to life.

It extended outward at both ends. From the upper end, a purple energy formed two curved, crescent-like blades. The lower end glowed with a small sphere of violet light.

A true alien weapon.

And the creature wielding it was a master.

The Artran warriors didn't stand a chance. Two of them lost their heads in a blur of motion. A third was struck by the glowing sphere—flung into a wall with a sickening crunch as its hollow bones shattered.

The fourth got a couple of shots off—but I heard the pinging sound of rounds ricocheting off metal. I couldn't force the vision to look down and see what armor I was wearing. I was just along for the ride.

Then the vision shifted. I was now an observer, watching Director Lorna and two soldiers place the alien weapon on the pedestal.

"This will go nicely with the set of Ghost armor we just acquired," she said. "I think Jack will be easy to control. After all, we gave him his life back."

She approached a cylinder built into the wall. There was a keypad—but she walked away before using it. The vision ended.

***

I was back in my body, the alien weapon still in my hand. It hadn't activated—yet.

But I closed my eyes, trying to recall the energy blades from the vision.

The weapon responded.

It came alive in my palm. The handle grew warm, the energy blades forming at each end. I could feel their power.

This thing could probably cut through any metal, I thought. *No wonder it had sliced through Artran heads so easily.*

Experimenting, I pictured a single axe blade instead of two.

The weapon responded again—shifting its shape to match my thoughts.

Images of techniques, combat maneuvers, and applications flowed into my mind. I forced them aside. I had more immediate needs.

If my armor is here, I need it.

I approached the cylinder built into the wall—the one from Lorna's vision. I aimed a downward slash, careful not to hit anything critical.

The thin metal gave way instantly.

Below it, the legs of my armor became visible.

Another slice. Then another.

Piece by piece, I extracted the armor and began strapping it onto my body.

Finally, I placed the helmet on my head. The system powered up, and the familiar voice of M6 greeted me.

"Before I went offline, we were being carried to a ship."

"I know, M6," I said. "There's no time to catch you up. Right now, I need your help getting out of this place."

Chapter: Thirty-Eight

Passing by the bodies of the fallen men in the hallway, I took the time to relieve them of any weapons or extra ammo clips they might have had.

All I gained was an extra nine-millimeter clip with standard rounds and a rifle with a few shots left in it. At least the armor was functioning normally—I was fully phased out now, staggering through the halls with growing confidence.

"My bio-readings on your body, Captain, are not good. Have you been tortured during your imprisonment?"

"Not exactly," I said. "As I told you before, I'll explain everything once we get out of this mess. Any luck finding a map or a system you can hack into?"

"No. And while I am contained within this body, I am unable to perform any tests that might rule out an airborne toxin or viral factor responsible for what you've observed."

"If it were airborne or viral, I'm sure I would've been exposed—same as everyone else."

"Then that leaves the possibility of a telepathic attack."

"No, no, no," I muttered. *If they took Ethan's body... What if he's not dead yet?*

"That is a possibility. Due to the damage to the armor systems and my placement, I cannot confirm. But if you've both been here for months, why now? Why today? Ethan would've used his ability to escape long ago."

"I don't know," I said, stepping into the lift. Bloodstains covered the walls and floor—but no bodies.

When the doors opened again, I found myself facing a hallway with flickering lights and smeared trails of blood across the tile. Phased out, I didn't worry about being seen or heard, so I moved forward, pistol raised, ready to fire—just in case I was wrong.

Eventually, the hallway ended at a promenade level, with wide openings looking down into a lower section. Polished marble floors reflected the soft, flickering light from overhead.

Below, water churned, fed by a waterfall pouring from a wall. I walked to the railing. There were steps leading down to the lower level, but I took the ones ascending through the center, climbing higher.

I was making a strong assumption that Director Lorna's office would be up this way. M6 backed me up with a 78% probability that I was right.

I passed through a set of glass doors marked with a strange Z slashed into a lightning bolt symbol. Inside was an open office area— where dozens of people had once worked.

Now, there was just a pile of bodies stacked in the center of the room.

Some had been shot. Others strangled. A few were hacked apart—likely not by the alien weapon I carried, but perhaps by a fire axe or machete.

"This is starting to look more and more like a telepathic attack from Ethan," I said aloud.

"These are all sadistic murders," M6 replied. "Not the methodical killings observed in Novick City."

"I know," I said grimly. "Maybe he's gone completely psychotic."

"That is a possibility. However, until we have further proof of Ethan's involvement, I will continue evaluating other explanations."

I passed through a pair of wooden doors. I knew I was getting close.

A desk stood off to the side. The next door bore the word **DIRECTOR** in a glowing digital display.

No handle.

But it had been left unlatched.

I pushed it open, sweeping the room with my weapon—no threats.

The director was slumped in her chair, her head resting on the desk.

Lifting her slightly by the hair, I saw that her neck had been snapped. Her dark blue eyes stared blankly at the wall-mounted screen to my left.

Someone on the monitor was waving frantically at the camera, screaming—but no sound played.

Then the person stepped back far enough for me to recognize her: Sophia. Still in that black dress. She was in what looked like a medical recovery room—larger than the one I'd woken in.

"Where is she?" I asked.

M6 responded. "She is on the second level, where you previously came from. Judging by the labeling system of the other cameras, this room is at the far end of the hallway opposite the armory."

"Why is she locked in there? Can you identify the communications system?"

"I have located it," M6 said, highlighting the back right hand portion of the director's desk. A large blood-stained blade was sticking out from it.

"That's not going to help," I said. "There's probably another panel nearby—maybe at the assistant's desk."

"I agree," M6 replied. "Unfortunately, she may not have much time. I have analyzed her lip movements and body language. I conclude that life support has been disabled in her section."

"Then we need to get her out," I said immediately.

"Captain, I must remind you—if Ethan is involved, this is likely a trap. Letting the woman die may be the better option."

M6 was right. It *was* probably a trap.

But so many people had already died. I could at least try to save *one*.

"We're saving her, M6," I said, turning and sprinting back toward the lift. "Unless you can tell me how to restore life support, I've got another way to get her out."

"Without knowing the full layout of this facility or what was done to the life support, I have nothing to offer," M6 replied.

I hoped I was doing the right thing.

Some part of me *knew* this was a trap.

But I didn't care.

I was going to save Sophia.

I wasn't going to let Ethan destroy another innocent life.

He'd already taken Jericho. He'd already cost millions of lives on Mars.

I couldn't atone for any of it.

But I could try to make a difference.

Chapter: Thirty-Nine

By the time I reached the door Sophia was behind, a new problem had presented itself.

"Base reactor is going critical," a female voice—very similar to Lorna's—announced over the now silent hallways. "All personnel are to evacuate immediately."

"How long do you think that gives us?" I asked.

"Depends on what was done to cause the critical state," M6 replied.

"So if you had to guess?" I asked, pulling the alien weapon from one of the armor's side pouches.

"My information is based on facts and data. I have none, and therefore cannot provide an answer."

"Ten minutes then," I said, forming a powerful energy axe head and smashing into the door. In less than a minute, I had carved a gap large enough for me to squat through.

"Sophia," I called out.

Everything in the room had begun to frost over, and a thick mist lingered in the air. My suit registered the temperature which had dropped to eighteen degrees—and it was still falling.

I found Sophia wrapped in several blankets, curled up on a hospital bed. Her body trembled as I scooped her into my arms.

What kind of surgeries had they been doing here? There were still so many unanswered questions about this place. If I just had more time, I could've learned what they had done to Ethan.

"You now have ten minutes to evacuate the facility," the female voice repeated.

"See, M6? Plenty of time."

By the time I reached the lift, I could no longer carry Sophia. I was completely exhausted—physically and mentally. All I wanted now was to sit down and enjoy a hot bowl of soup.

When the lift doors opened, I dragged Sophia in. Her eyes were open now, looking up at me from the floor.

"Can you stand?" I asked.

She didn't speak, but reached out a shaking hand and pulled herself up. Once she was stable against the wall, I grabbed the blankets and draped them back over her shoulders.

"You now have six minutes to evacuate," the voice announced again.

"We need to hurry," I said, staggering along the corridor. We were both weak. It took everything we had, working together, to navigate the hallways and reach the stairs.

"There should still be some ships in the main bay?" I asked.

She nodded.

When we finally arrived, the voice announced: "Three minutes remaining."

Several freighter ships sat in the bay, but only one had its cargo ramp lowered.

I led us toward that one, half-expecting resistance, but we encountered no one. No guards. No crew. Nothing.

Whatever Ethan had done—it had been sadistic and outright evil.

It gave me pause: why had I been spared? And more importantly, why Sophia?

"I like this ship already," M6 said. "Its security is so outdated I've already gained full access to all onboard systems."

"That's great, M6. Now stop talking and let's get the hell out of here," I said, helping Sophia into the co-pilot's seat. Once she was buckled in, I took the pilot's chair.

"All systems are powered and ready. Bay doors are open and the forcefield is stable for exit."

Had another vessel already escaped before us? Was that why the doors were open?

I had no time to investigate. M6 reported two minutes to critical. We barely had enough time to clear the facility.

I pulled back on the control stick, guiding the ship through the shimmering blue forcefield. Outside, we entered a narrow canyon, ascending between jagged cliffs while a heavy snowstorm raged around us.

My plan had been to hit full acceleration as soon as we cleared the bay—but the storm reduced visibility to almost nothing. And flying at high speed through a canyon during a blizzard was suicide.

When the shockwave from the explosion hit us, the ship was slammed from behind. The engines failed. The vessel spun into a spiraling free fall.

The control stick was useless. Without power, the inertial dampers were offline, and G-forces slammed me back into my seat.

"Re-igniting engines now," M6 said.

The lights flickered. The dampers powered up.

I seized the stick again, fighting against the controls, trying to break our dive. But we scraped the top of a snow-covered mountain before I managed to stabilize us—barely.

"I need more power to the engines!" I shouted.

"A few more seconds, Captain!"

"We don't have them!" I yelled, as the ship clipped another mountaintop.

Sophia screamed beside me. Honestly, I wanted to scream too—we were going down, fast.

"M6!" I snapped.

Just then, the engines roared back to life. I pulled hard on the stick, trying to lift the ship out of the plunge. The blizzard outside obscured everything. I was flying blind.

We skimmed terrifyingly close to the ground. Then I saw it— a rocky outcropping dead ahead.

I rolled the vessel sharply to the right, just missing it.

Sophia screamed again. My heart pounded in my chest.

At last, we cleared the canyon and burst into open sky.

We reached space.

I cut the engines and let the vessel coast. My hands trembled on the controls. I had no idea where to go or what to do next.

It was time to get some answers.

"How are you doing?" I asked, glancing at Sophia. She was still clinging to the blankets.

"Getting warmer," she said weakly. "So…what's the plan?"

"That's what I was hoping you could tell me," I said. "How did you end up trapped in that room, while everyone else was killing each other?"

Without hesitation, she answered. "I was visiting a patient—someone who'd just come out of surgery."

"Who?" I asked.

She gave me a blank look, then squinted, as if struggling to remember. "I don't know. I just remember someone touching my face…and then I woke up on the bed, freezing."

"She's telling the truth," M6 said. "Heart rate and eye dilation are consistent with honesty."

"Was the patient Ethan?"

"I don't think so. We have so many clients…"

Time to change tactics.

"What exactly does Zytec specialize in?"

A small smile touched her lips. "We find cures for incurable diseases. We run programs to slow aging. Zytec's mission is to eradicate disease and extend the human lifespan."

"So…are you one of Zytec's experiments?"

She looked away for a moment, then turned back. "Yes. And that's all I'll say about it."

"Fine," I said. "Do you know where I can get more of that drug Lorna said I need every couple of days?"

"The corporate headquarters. On Earth."

"Not going back there unless I have no other choice. So how do I cure what they did to me?"

"You don't," she said flatly. "How else do you think they keep control of us?"

Wait. That meant…

"You need the drug too?"

"Of course. I'm property, just like you, Jack. But unlike you, I owe Zytec everything—my life, my health, my career."

"I'm sorry," I said. "I get it. You have your reasons. But I want no part in this."

I removed my helmet and gloves.

I didn't know exactly what I was about to do. But I needed answers—answers only someone like Sophia, a personal assistant to Director Lorna, might have.

There had to be a cure.

I didn't have time to play twenty questions to find it.

I didn't even know if my telepathic abilities would respond the way they had in the past. The alien artifact had triggered the first vision I'd had since waking from the coma.

To read someone or something, I needed a clear mind and a focused intention.

"What are you doing?" she demanded, as I leaned toward her, cupping her face in my hands.

I looked into her eyes.

And the world shifted.

***

I was an invisible observer inside a medical room I didn't recognize—definitely not part of the Zytec facility I'd escaped.

Director Lorna and Sophia stood with two technicians beside a strange cylindrical device that dominated the center of the room.

Strange symbols lined the edges—symbols I recognized as belonging to the Ancients.

Director Lorna spoke. "Tell us about this device."

One of the technicians stepped forward—his hood removed, revealing a bushy black beard. He placed a hand on the dull gray surface.

"Director," he said, "we call it the *Medusa*. And I think you'll be very pleased with what it does."

Chapter: Forty

Director Lorna stepped closer to the alien machine and placed her palm on it.

"You've chosen an interesting name for it. I'm intrigued."

The technician gave her a grin before continuing.
"This device was recovered from the shielded city during the recent conflict between the Nomads and the invaders from the portal the Ancients left behind."

Lorna waved her hand dismissively.
"Don't bore me with a history lesson. I'm well aware of current galactic affairs. Just tell me what the thing does."

"Sorry, Director," the man said, stepping back from the machine. "It took us a few days to get it open, but inside was an ancient being. Unfortunately, it was already dead. We believe it died almost instantly after the machine was taken offline."

"Interesting," Lorna mused. "A fresh biological sample of an Ancient is a worthy find in itself. Full viral protocols were taken, I trust?"

"Indeed," the technician replied. "We took no chances being exposed to whatever degenerative plague wiped them out. After the body was removed and sent to Earth for study, we decontaminated the machine and began our investigation."

Lorna slowly circled the machine, running her hands along its surface.

"The *Medusa* is a miracle device," the technician said. "It can reverse genetic deterioration and repair cells and organs. Then, through a process we haven't fully understood, it freezes them in that state. We don't know how long the effect lasts, but we estimate it kept that Ancient alive for thousands of years."

Lorna stopped and smiled broadly.
"A miracle device indeed. Does it work on humans?"

"It's worked on everything we've tested so far. The Medusa performs a full biological scan of the subject, learns everything it needs to, then goes to work."

"It makes you wonder," Lorna said, placing both hands on the device, "how in the hell were the Ancients defeated?"

The room fell silent.

And then I felt myself being pulled backward.

The vision faded, and I stood before Sophia, my hands frozen just inches from her face.

"You had no right to that information," she snapped, crossing her arms.

"The *Medusa*—is that the device the Voidborn stole?" I asked, already certain of the answer.

After a pause and averted glance, she finally responded.
"It is. That's what Lorna wanted you to recover."

"And will it cure my condition?"

Her gaze turned sharp, arms still crossed.
"Yes."

I was surprised she wasn't using her pheromones to manipulate me. Then again, nothing about how she survived the colony made sense.

I sat in the pilot's chair and swiveled to face her.

"I know we don't trust each other, but if I'm going to recover this device, we need to start working together. That is…if you still care about the device."

I wished I still had my neural link with M6. He could detect signs of lying or evasion. He could still do it with my helmet on—but wearing it now wouldn't help with building trust.

"The recovery of the device is top priority," she said flatly.

"Then we're partners in this. Once I recover it and cure myself, you're free to go. Deal?"

"Deal," she said, arms still crossed. "But the first priority is securing more *Tripozine*. The only place to get that now is on Earth."

"I'm not going back to Earth," I said.

"You're not a wanted man anymore, Jack. Facial, retina, and biometric scans will register you as Patrick Jackson Howard of the Corin Colony. Zytec has a deal with them."

"And they don't have the drug?"

"No. It's highly regulated and can only be manufactured by Zytec."

"How long before it starts wearing off?"

"I had a recent injection," she said, finally uncrossing her arms. "You, on the other hand, haven't had one since yesterday. That gives me about seventy-three hours before I feel the first symptoms."

"So I've got about twenty-four?"

She nodded.

"Nothing like a tight deadline to keep you motivated," I said. "So…how do we find these pirates?"

"You don't find them," she said, lowering her voice. "They find you."

She was right. The Voidborn were elusive. I knew from prior intelligence that several pirates had defected to the CEF, but their info never led us to the base.

I picked my helmet off the floor and slipped it back on.

"M6," I said, "have you been monitoring the conversation?"

"I have," came the reply. "And I've gained full access to the ship's systems."

"Good. Route yourself through the internal speakers. We're going to have a strategy session—with Sophia."

Just before removing the helmet, I asked, "Have you done a bioscan on her?"

"Everything checks out. Minor frostbite on some areas, but nothing the onboard medkit can't handle."

"Keep monitoring her. Especially her biochemistry. She's used pheromones on me in the past."

"Understood, Captain."

I removed the helmet. Sophia was still watching me with that same unreadable expression.

I felt like I was being played.

"M6, can you hear me?"

"Loud and clear, Captain," came his voice over the speakers. "How can I help?"

"How current are your files on the Voidborn pirate organization?"

"I'm missing the last year's worth of data. But based on what I have, there's a 20% probability the pirate base has been located."

"What's our best course of action to find it?"

A holographic projection flickered to life, displaying the dark, volatile region known as the Golar Nebula—a chaotic expanse of ion storms and rogue asteroids whipped by cosmic forces.

"One of the most recent incidents involved the theft of the *CEF Dawson* and the kidnapping of Admiral Frost. His report includes coordinates for a planet inside the nebula—used by the pirates."

"How is that possible?" I asked. "This nebula was formed by the collision of two supernovas. There shouldn't be habitable worlds in there."

"There is a 30% chance of habitable systems existing within isolated pockets of the nebula," M6 replied.

"Then we start there. That planet—"

"You two aren't serious, are you?" Sophia cut in, giving me a pointed look.

"It's a good place to start," I said. "Hell, the pirates probably still operate from there."

"There are too many *what ifs* in your plan, Jack. I have a better one."

"A few seconds ago, you didn't even know where to look. So why the sudden insight?"

She smirked.
"First, I wanted to see what kind of intel you had on the pirates. Second, I wanted to see how you'd plan to find them. And honestly? I'm disappointed."

Great. Now she was scolding me like a schoolteacher.

"You do know what I used to do for the CEF, right?" I asked.

"Of course I do. That's why I expected a better plan. Mine is simpler. And guaranteed to get their attention."

"Care to share it?"

"No," she said flatly. "Set course for the Crayor System."

I stared at her.

It took effort to unclench my fingers from the armrest. After a few deep breaths, I focused again.

Sophia knew more than she was letting on. She had some past connection to the pirates. That much was obvious. She was far too confident for someone making a guess—especially when she needed the drug as badly as I did.

Taking another breath, I gave the order.

"M6, set course for Crayor."

A few seconds later, the stars elongated into streaks of light through the transparasteel window as we jumped to hyperspace. I leaned back in the chair.

I needed food. I needed sleep. But most of all, I needed answers.

Except I couldn't relax.

I didn't trust this woman. Not for a second.

Her survival, her vague memories, her connection to the *Medusa*—none of it added up.

But I would find out the truth.

That, I swore to myself.

Chapter: Forty-One

At some point, I had dozed off. When I opened my eyes again, Sophia was standing next to me, holding a steaming bowl of some kind of soup.

I had given M6 instructions to keep an eye on her. He should've alerted me to her movements.

"You need to eat, Jack," she said. "I'm surprised you're as active as you are after that starvation gambit you pulled."

"It wasn't a gambit," I said, taking the bowl from her. It was warm to the touch, and the scent hit me almost instantly—chicken broth, onions, mushrooms.

Sophia returned to her seat as I called out to M6. "What's our ETA?"

"Three hours and fifteen minutes," M6 responded.

Just hearing his voice confirmed she hadn't deactivated him during my sleep. I looked down at the bowl, searching for a spoon, but found none.

When I looked over at Sophia, she was already watching me, miming the action of drinking from an invisible bowl.

If it weren't for the growling in my stomach, I might have refused. But instead, I slowly drank the liquid. It took restraint. My first instinct was to gulp it down.

"You really are very disciplined," she noted.

I said nothing—just kept drinking. When I finished, I rested the bowl in my lap.

Sophia broke the silence.
"While you were sleeping, M6 showed me images of what happened at Zytec. I was shocked by the horror of it all. And I've come to one conclusion."

I sat up straighter, hopeful for some truth.

"You weren't the only one rescued from the *Kuroseki*," she said.

"Was Ethan still alive?" I asked. A cold dread washed over me, like ice water pouring down my spine. Every muscle tensed.

"Yes," she said with a nod.

"You knew what kind of monster he was—and you still saved him?" My fingers dug into the armrest.

It was unthinkable. But it made everything that had happened make sense.

"I was under orders to retrieve him," she said. "Zytec believed they could contain and control him."

"Obviously not," I muttered.

She continued, unfazed.
"At first, he was compliant. Defiant at times, but cooperative. Lorna believed he could be an asset to the company—especially with his telepathic abilities. So, we patched up his body and made some enhancements."

"Enhancements?" I asked. The word alone was enough to raise alarm bells.

"If you didn't know," she explained, "Zytec began as a company specializing in cloning organs for clients. The goal was to transfer consciousness to a cloned body. When that failed, they partnered with Omicron Technologies to experiment with hybrid bodies."

I'd heard rumors. Injured vets receiving realistic-looking synthetic limbs. Tech that blurred the line between man and machine.

"We patented a process that allows human skin to be grown over hybrid parts," she said. "Eventually, we could transplant a functioning human brain into a full hybrid body. Turns out, blending biology and mechanics was easier than expected."

"You didn't…you didn't put his *brain* in one of those machine bodies, did you?" I asked, horrified at the mental image of a half-man, half-machine abomination.

"No," she said. "But he agreed to have his arms and legs replaced with cybernetic limbs. He can run faster, jump higher, crush steel pipes with his hands. We also installed ballistic plating to protect his vital organs."

I clenched my jaw. I wanted to rage. Instead, I forced myself to breathe.

"And now the monster's loose again," I said. "He manipulated all of you into doing his bidding. You should've let him die. I should have."

She said nothing in return.

We sat in silence as the ship approached the planet. I tried not to think about Ethan. There would be time for him later.

For now, the priority was the cure.

***

Crayor was one of the first Earth-like worlds to be colonized. In its early days, it boasted advanced technology. Engineers had designed a power system that tapped into the planet's thermal core, bringing limitless energy to a rapidly growing city.

Now, as I glided over the ruins of that once-great metropolis, I saw no sign of human life. Just vegetation creeping up the steel bones of skyscrapers, preparing to entomb them in nature's quiet reclamation.

The surviving colonists had relocated to the pristine white coasts, building modest settlements powered by the sea. It was rumored that the first leaders of the Voidborn pirate organization hailed from Crayor, during the early days of the Artran conflict.

And it was noted—at least in intelligence circles—that this system was rarely raided, unlike other human colonies nearby. Many believed the people of Crayor still had deep ties to the Voidborn.

"Three minutes to landing," M6 reported.

"Ever been to Crayor before?" Sophia asked, sitting at the edge of her seat, gazing through the transparasteel window at the sprawling coastline below.

"Just in pictures and vids," I replied.

"The water is so clear you can see for miles beneath the surface," she said wistfully. "There's a massive variety of sea life— more than one person could study in a lifetime."

"With the war over," I offered, "maybe that life could still be yours."

Her smile faded.

"We all have our duties," she said. "And the war isn't over. That telepathic blast you sent out—it just exposed the Artran empire for what it really is."

That "telepathic blast" had been mentioned several times now, but I couldn't recall it.
No images. No sensations. Just what Lorna had told me.

"Sorry," I said. "I keep hearing about this blast, but I have no memory of it—just what Lorna said."

Her eyes met mine.

"When it happened, it was the scariest moment in human history. For a brief few seconds, everyone in the galaxy—*everyone*—froze."

"Were people killed?" I asked.

"No. But the images you shared—Ethan nuking the Mars colony, the Artrans raising the dead to fight—it all lasted maybe two or three seconds, but it felt like minutes."

Her gaze dropped to the floor as the ship began to descend.

She looked up again.

"Near the end, all the images merged into one: the Artrans marching through the streets of Earth. Fire everywhere. No humans resisted. They were frozen in place, like statues."

"A warning about the future?" I asked.

She nodded.

"I'm surprised the CEF didn't just declare war again," I said as I heard the ramp lowering at the rear of the ship. Waves crashed in the distance. Birds sang.

"They would've," she replied. "But the Artrans received the message too. It caused political upheaval in their empire. There's a civil war now, within the ruling caste. The CEF is waiting—rebuilding—until a victor emerges."

So the telepathic warning had worked—just like the beings in the Omega Mirror said it would. It had bought us time.

Sophia stood and looked out the window again, smiling.
"For my plan to work, you'll need to stay cloaked and close to me. Do not break cloak until I say so."

I was about to argue, but she handed me my helmet.
"Now let's go. We're running out of time."

Once again, I was following her into the unknown. Her confidence gave me just enough reason to trust her—for now. I locked the helmet into place.

"Keep a watch, M6," I said as we stepped into the golden light of a beautiful summer morning. Tall green trees stretched in every direction. The dirt paths were little more than trails cut through undergrowth.

As we neared civilization, I realized it was nothing more than a village made of wooden buildings and reed-thatched roofs. Tech was minimal, though I could hear the quiet hum of cooling systems here and there.

Sophia moved through the village with ease. Everyone watched her. Most were armed—pistols, shotguns, a few rifles slung over shoulders.

Our journey ended at a bar with open walls and ceiling fans lazily spinning above. There were pool tables off to the right and dozens of people drinking and chatting.

Sophia took a few steps inside and raised her voice.

"I'm looking for James Howardson. He needs to know—I'm carrying his child."

The room fell silent.

All eyes turned to her.

What the hell had she just said?

And was it even true?

Chapter: Forty-Two

Murmurs began to ripple through the patrons of the bar. From what few whispers I could catch, the focus was squarely on Sophia. It was clear she was a familiar face around here.

"M6," I asked, "did your most recent bioscan of Sophia reveal a pregnancy?"

As I waited for his response, the aged bartender motioned for Sophia to come toward him. I followed.

"The pregnancy results are inconclusive," M6 said. "If she is still early in her first trimester, I would require a blood sample to be one hundred percent accurate."

"I'm sure she'll agree to that," I muttered, now standing behind her.

The bartender's skin was dark and leathery, his head shaved bald. He wore a stained leather apron over his broad chest and belly.

Sophia leaned in as the man spoke to her. M6 enhanced the audio so I could hear.

"James will be back tonight," the bartender said. "I have the key to his cabin. I think it's best you have that conversation in private."

He handed her a key, and just like that, we were walking back out of the bar, heading toward the edge of town.

"M6, do you have an analysis of this place for me?"

My helmet's visor dimmed as an aerial map was displayed. Even from the sky, it was obvious this town wasn't as populated as it first appeared.

"I estimate about ten thousand residents in this settlement," M6 said. "There is very little active technology, so I have nothing to hack into."

"Should we launch the trackers to locate this Howardson?"

"No need," M6 replied. "Based on the bar conversations, I've concluded the person in question is off-world, conducting some kind of legitimate trade for the colonists."

"Did anything turn up in CEF records?"

"It did. If this is Jackson Howardson, then he was drafted early in the war as a pilot. He mostly transported troops and supplies, but near the end of his career, he was being trained to fly bulk cruisers in combat."

"What happened to him?"

"During the conflict at Planet 2186, he was shot down by Artran forces and spent several weeks behind enemy lines with a small squad. He was the only survivor. Despite severe injuries, he made it back and recovered. A few months later, he was discharged for mental health concerns. I don't have the full report, but his debriefing suggests he and several others were captured and tortured by an Artran team."

"At least now we know a little about who we're dealing with," I said, as Sophia stopped at the door to a small shack at the edge of the jungle, overlooking the coast. I could hear the waves crashing nearby.

She glanced back at me, then opened the door.

The inside was cozy. A large bed sat beside a wide window with a stunning view of the ocean. There were a couple of chairs crafted from local wood, a small kitchen area with a wooden bar, and a compact refrigeration unit. No entertainment systems—just a bookshelf filled with well-worn books.

Sophia went straight to the fridge and pulled out two bottles. She found a glass beneath the bar and began mixing them.

Phasing in, I appeared across from her at the bar. "You know, a woman in your condition shouldn't be drinking."

She took a long swig before slamming the glass down. "After the day I've had, I deserve it. And what happened to our agreement that you wouldn't come out of cloak until I said so?"

"You realize I've got limited energy reserves, and this place isn't exactly crawling with recharging points."

She walked to one of the chairs and sat down, drink in hand. "These people have suffered unimaginable loss during the war. It's amazing anyone still lives here."

"I don't know," I said, taking the other chair. "The scenery grows on you. If you're looking for a no-tech, laid-back lifestyle, this place is paradise."

"So is it true?" I asked.

She took another sip. "Is what true?"

"Your pregnancy," I said, raising my voice slightly.

She shrugged. "It's more of a maybe than anything."

Why couldn't she just give me a straight answer?

M6 cut in, "Enhanced audio has detected multiple individuals approaching the cabin. They're discussing tactics to capture Sophia."

Before I could react, she reached out and touched my armored wrist.

"No matter how bad this gets, stay close to me and do not reveal yourself unless absolutely necessary." She pulled her arm back just as M6 activated phasing. The door slammed open.

Five armed men and one green-skinned lizard alien stormed in. I was already on my feet, shifting along the wall, invisible.

I recognized the alien species immediately. The CEF had nicknamed them Nomads—spacefaring wanderers who had drifted into CEF territory. After capture and eventual translation breakthroughs, they were conscripted into the war effort and granted a homeworld. That world had since died when its atmosphere generator was destroyed.

The leader was a tall, muscular Black man with a few missing teeth. He carried a shortened shotgun over his shoulder and got right in Sophia's face.

"Good to see you again," he said. "And congrats on the pregnancy. James will be thrilled."

"I know he will," Sophia said calmly. "So where is he?"

He stuck a toothpick in his mouth and chewed it before answering.
"There's just one problem, Sophia."

"And that is, Bernard?"

He grinned. "That ship you arrived in—we know it belonged to the Chadwick brothers. And they were working with Zytec."

"Okay…and the question is?"

Bernard spit the toothpick onto the floor.
"Where are the Chadwick brothers?"

Sophia looked around at the group.
"They're dead. Zytec's colony was destroyed."

"And how do you know this?" Bernard asked, stepping closer.

"Because I worked for Zytec."

The words barely left her lips before one of the men threw a black sack over her head and restrained her arms. They dragged her from the cabin.

There was no time to question anything—I had to follow.

They led her through the village and into the jungle, where a freighter ship waited.

I had no choice but to board with them. They secured Sophia in a small crew cabin. I stayed phased in a dark corner, watching and listening.

"Any idea where we're headed?" I asked.

"There's a high probability we're being taken to the pirate hideout," M6 replied. "Every crew member on this freighter is registered as a known Voidborn."

"Well, at least Sophia's plan is working," I said.

"It will not end the way she hopes," M6 replied. "I've overheard multiple crew members say Howardson is dead."

"Well, shit," I said, tightening my grip on my rifle.

Chapter: Forty-Three

About an hour into the voyage, I found a maintenance closet near the cargo bay with a functioning power outlet. It wasn't enough to keep the suit running at a sustainable sixty-eight percent. I would have to come out of phase to charge—and this closet seemed like a temporary safe shelter to do just that.

Barring the door with a mop handle, I disengaged the phasing system and propped myself against the wall to wait. I really wished there was something to sit on. My only option was the floor, knees pulled to my chest like some tired prisoner.

Depending on how long this mission dragged on—and I was confident it would last more than two or three days—sleep and food were going to become real problems. I'd already rummaged through my utility cylinder for ration bars and caffeine pills, but Zytec had clearly failed to stock any.

After an hour of standing, I gave in and dropped to the floor.

"M6," I said, "how's your attempt to hack their system going?"

"No progress," M6 replied. "Despite the outdated equipment the pirates are using, they've managed to construct an almost impenetrable computer system."

"I've got one spike left, but I think I'll hold on to that for now."

"Agreed," M6 said. "With the aid of the trackers, I've been monitoring Sophia and the crew."

"How are they treating her?" I asked.

M6 projected a live feed from one of the tracker spheres. Sophia had been placed in a small cabin and was pacing with a steaming cup in hand. After a minute or so, she sat on the edge of a single bed, picked up a well-worn hardback book from the floor, and began reading.

She didn't appear to be in immediate danger.

"Have you learned anything else?" I asked.

"In several overheard conversations, I've gathered that this crew was responsible for stealing the *Medusa* from Zytec."

That gave me pause. This ragtag group had basic weapons, minimal body armor, and none of the discipline of a special ops team. They certainly didn't act like the terrifying force I'd heard described in survivor debriefs—mist-filled corridors, monsters, and demons immune to bullets and fire.

Of course, those stories made more sense after toxicology reports revealed that survivors had been exposed to a powerful, unidentified hallucinogen. The mist, monsters, and demons were all consistent accounts. It was clear that the pirates' main tactic was to flood the ship with gas before boarding—softening up the resistance with fear and confusion. Smart. It also reduced the number of attackers needed for a successful takeover.

Still, my thoughts kept drifting back to Zytec. With the kind of mercenaries they could afford to hire, this merry little band shouldn't have stood a chance.

M6 continued, "It was also mentioned that they had help from an insider."

"Do you know who it was?" I asked, immediately suspecting Sophia. She already had ties to the Voidborn, and truthfully, I had no idea where her loyalties lay. She might be working with the Voidborn—and with Ethan—helping him escape. A knot of questions twisted in my gut. Years of training had taught me how to unravel that knot: ask the right questions, and the truth would follow.

First question: if Sophia was the traitor, why stay at Zytec? Once her deception was uncovered, she'd be an easy target. Unless…she had someone else do her bidding. With her pheromone attractant and someone's desire to possess her, betrayal wouldn't be hard to coax.

The problem was, M6 didn't have access to employee files or detailed records of the pirate raid. All I needed was for one of the pirates to slip up and name someone. That would start the unraveling.

With that question still unresolved, I moved on.

Second question: why defect now?

The answer came faster than expected—and it chilled me. If the *Medusa* could sever Zytec's control over its operatives, now would be the perfect time for her to escape. And if Ethan was her weapon of choice for that escape? It was almost elegant in its simplicity.

So why bring me along?

The answer was equally simple. She wasn't a true defector. I was here to help her steal the *Medusa* and disappear—into a safe haven I was sure she'd already arranged.

That new understanding of Sophia forced me to pause and reset. This was a dangerous woman—one willing to let others die to reach her goals.

I considered going over my reasoning again to ensure I wasn't biasing my conclusions. But I didn't get the chance.

Someone began pushing aggressively against the door.

Phasing out, I quickly rose and drew my pistol. The rifle was strapped to my chest, but in tight quarters like this, a sidearm would serve me better.

The mop handle gave way with a snap, and the door burst open.

For the briefest moment, a green-skinned Nomad stood framed in the doorway, rifle aimed directly at me. Its snout tilted slightly upward, nostrils flaring. Even though it couldn't see me, it knew I was there. I could hear deep inhalations—it was sampling the air.

It could smell me.

I had forgotten how acute their olfactory senses were. Phasing couldn't hide that.

I pulled the trigger.

Chapter: Forty-Four

I had forgotten how quick Nomads could be. We both fired at the same time. I heard the impact of bullets striking my chest plate. My pistol shots winged the Nomad's shoulder, but it rolled away from the doorway and vanished down the narrow corridor.

It would only be seconds before the whole ship was alerted to my presence—and there was no telling what kind of gear this crew had.

What were my options?

"M6, bring the spheres closer to my position. I need a tactical update. How are the pirates organizing to root me out?"

"I have already directed one to follow the Nomad," M6 replied. "It made a straight run for the mess hall, where the largest congregation of crew is located. Three of them—including the Nomad—are now moving down the corridor toward your position. Two others have gone in the opposite direction."

"Any special equipment? Gravimetric sensors?" I asked.

"No. May I suggest heading toward the rear cargo bay? You'll have ample room to hide and strike."

"That's the obvious plan, M6. I think I'll pay a visit to this nearby room. According to your makeshift map, it's a crew quarters. Also, bring one of the spheres to me. I have a use for it."

"After quick analysis, I conclude you intend an unorthodox method of subterfuge," M6 said.

I didn't have time to respond. I was lucky the door was unlocked. I slipped inside and shut it softly behind me.

The room was dim, lit only by a single wall light above the door. The bed and floor were cluttered with worn clothing. A makeshift chemistry set sat on a table, with several blue-stained cylinders nearby.

If I had to guess, this Voidborn was manufacturing illegal substances—but I didn't have time to investigate. M6 had already pulled up a video feed of the Nomad-led team approaching down the corridor.

"Where's my sphere?" I asked, removing a lower armor plate from between my legs. I grabbed one of the larger beakers on the table and relieved myself—just enough to douse the sphere that had just flown through a vent and landed in my palm.

Wasting no time, I poured the contents over the sphere and ordered M6 to send it back through the ventilation system toward the cargo bay.

Then I threw on one of the pirate's shirts and wrapped a filthy sock around my hand. On the feed, I saw the Nomad pause near the door, sniff the air, then take off down the corridor—passing the maintenance closet I'd previously hidden in.

"So far, so good," I muttered. "M6, send the other sphere from Sophia's tracker to monitor the second team the Nomad alerted."

"On it," M6 replied, just as I cracked the door open to scan the hallway. All clear.

The second video feed came online, showing the other group on the bridge, yelling at each other. Even with audio enhancement, it was difficult to make out exact words, but it was clear—they were blaming each other for letting a ghost operative onboard.

"M6, move that feed to the lower-right corner. Put the cargo bay feed in the upper-left. My little distraction seems to be working." M6 had positioned the sphere high up in the bay, giving me a good vantage point of the pirates spread out and searching.

"Now to close this can of sardines," I said, moving swiftly down the corridor toward the far end.

I reached the cargo bay control panel and began entering commands to seal and lock the doors—only for the digital display to go dark.

"Something's happening," M6 said, enlarging the cargo bay feed.

I glanced at it—two pirates were looking toward the door I was standing at.

The Nomad wasn't among them.

That's because he was right in front of me.

He emerged silently from a blind spot, rifle raised, ready to fire at point-blank range.

My rifle was strapped across my chest—no room to bring it up—so I lashed out with my right leg in a stomping motion, aiming for the Nomad's stomach.

But again, its speed was unnerving. It twisted mid-move and barreled into me, knocking us both to the ground.

I landed hard on my back, and suddenly it was on top of me. Where the hell had it pulled that small axe from? It was raised above my head, ready to strike.

The Nomad growled something unintelligible.

I didn't wait for a translation.

I jabbed two fingers at the vulnerable point of its neck—Nomads, like humans, had windpipes. I missed, barely grazing the scaly hide.

It roared and drove its whole body into the downward axe strike.

My other arm swung up fast—my elbow slammed into the alien's lower jaw. The axe missed my head, glancing off my helmet and smashing into the metal grate beside me.

Off balance now, I heaved it over my head.

It wasn't clean—it grabbed my rifle and snapped it from its sling.

I scrambled to my feet just as the other two pirates appeared at the door and opened fire.

Bullets slammed into my armor. The built-in deflector was absorbing most of the impact, but my HUD showed the green barrier energy depleting fast.

My pistol was at my side—but my hand instinctively went to the alien weapon clipped to my belt. I drew it.

It pulsed in my grip.

The staff didn't fully extend—just a short, bo staff length rod with glowing orbs of energy at both ends.

I spun and struck.

The first pirate flew backwards, crashing into a crate with a loud thud.

The second rolled past me—quick—and as I turned, a powerful kick from behind sent me stumbling into the cargo bay.

I lost control of my body, but I let momentum carry me—I tucked and rolled.

Rolling in armor isn't easy, but I'd practiced enough to land on my feet.

I came up beside the unconscious pirate, facing the now-sealed cargo bay door. Red warning lights flashed across the walls.

"They're venting the bay," M6 announced—just as I felt myself yanked off the floor, sucked backward toward the opening airlock.

Out into the maelstrom of the nebula.

Chapter: Forty-Five

I was heading straight out the cargo bay door and into the maelstrom of a dark nebula. There were no twinkling stars to admire—only black, blue, and purple rolling clouds of gas streaked with ionized electrical discharges.

Once my body passed beyond the ship's deflector field, I'd be exposed to deadly levels of radiation—enough to kill me in minutes. I had come this far, and honestly, I didn't want it to end this way. I wanted to be with my family, but every time I looked death in the face, I was somehow pulled back into the fight.

Some would call it fate or destiny—and I was beginning to believe that fate still wanted something from me. How else could I explain the coincidence of a floating crate drifting alongside me, a strap entangled around my leg, keeping me just inside the vessel's deflector boundary?

I was too breathless to scream in relief. When I looked back at the cargo bay door, it had already closed. There was no going back that way.

Gripping the strap, I pulled myself toward the ship's hull and pressed my boots against the surface. They locked on with a satisfying click—magnetized. At least now I had some footing.

"Do you still have a sphere inside?" I asked.

M6 responded, "Signal clarity is poor, but from the crew's conversations, they believe you're dead."

"In reality, I should be," I muttered. "Alright, priority one—can you guide me to a panel that provides oxygen access?"

A red line appeared across my visor.

"I can do even better," M6 said. "There's a power conduit near one of the oxygen scrubbers."

"Any chance it'll trigger an internal alarm?"

"None. This ship was built during the early days of colonization. Back then, no one anticipated an external breach."

"Well, that's some good news. Have you reviewed our last encounter? Any idea what went wrong?"

"I've drawn my conclusions. The scenario with the highest probability points to an error on your part."

"So, yeah…pissing on the sphere was a bit much. It seemed like a great idea at the time," I said.

"It would've worked—if you hadn't entered the quarters of one of the men stationed on the bridge," M6 replied.

"How'd you figure that out?"

"Blue chemical stains on the clothing—same as the ones found in that makeshift chemistry lab. It wasn't obvious until you were already being attacked. The Nomad was playing along with your ruse to lure you into a trap. One of the audio logs from the sphere confirms an exchange between the Nomad and the captain."

"Okay, okay. I made a bad call. I didn't want to kill these people."

"They, on the other hand, had no such restrictions on violence," M6 said.

"Yeah, I noticed," I said, coming to a stop at the end of the red line. "I'd forgotten how fast and strong Nomads really are."

I waited for a reply, but M6 was now focused on guiding me through the process of opening the panel, rerouting power to my suit, and restoring oxygen flow.

As it stood, I could survive on the hull for maybe two hours before suffocating. I had no idea how long this ride would last.

Ships couldn't use jump space inside the nebula. They had to crawl through it—slow, hazardous, unpredictable.

The nebula had once been a buffer zone during the war—until the Voidborn claimed it as their own.

"You're doing great, Captain. The power conduit should fully recharge your suit. Let's move on to the oxygen line now."

Once oxygen began pumping into the suit, I flipped over onto my back and stared at the swirling storm around me. My thoughts drifted again—to Sophia. Was she manipulating everyone around her? I didn't have an answer yet.

***

Several hours later, M6 alerted me that the freighter was decelerating.

I stood up and looked around, but the nebula swallowed everything in its dangerous beauty. A minute later, the ship came to a full stop, and I could finally make out the vague outline of something massive beside us.

"Have you been able to identify it?" I asked, already suspecting the answer.

"No. You'll need to gather more data."

Unhooking myself from the freighter, I began the slow walk toward the new vessel. With my suit fully charged and everyone believing I was dead, I felt safer—though I still had to avoid the Nomads.

"They're moving Sophia off the freighter," M6 said. "The sphere is almost out of power. We could lose it at any time."

"Follow her as long as possible. When you can't, ditch the sphere somewhere they'll have a hard time finding it. We don't need them searching for me again."

"Understood. Interference has decreased," M6 reported.

"Enough to give me visual feed?"

My left-hand periphery lit up as the sphere transmitted footage of a crowded corridor. People were milling about, talking, or moving with purpose. It wasn't clear if this was a market or a residential zone.

Everyone was armed. Worn clothes, scuffed boots, no uniforms—just raw survival.

"Great," I muttered. "Just great. Operational nightmare."

I reached the edge of the freighter and found myself facing a massive wall of modified cargo containers. Below, I could just make out the docking port where our freighter had attached.

Even without seeing the whole thing, I knew what I was looking at—the pirates had converted a cargo vessel into a mobile base.

A rough estimate told me this ship could house ten thousand or more, given the scale.

If I wanted to get in unnoticed, the aft section was my best bet. Engine bays always had access hatches.

A few minutes later, M6 powered down the tracker sphere. He'd hidden it inside a ventilation shaft near where they'd taken Sophia.

My right-hand display lit up with a rudimentary map showing the route the sphere had taken. From the freighter to its final resting place, Sophia had passed through a crowded section and then taken a lift far up into what I suspected was the bridge.

Soon after, I reached a rusted manual access hatch—a classic turn-wheel model. M6 scanned it and gave the all-clear.

I gripped the wheel and twisted.

The hatch creaked open, revealing a dark shaft with a barely visible ladder descending into the black.

I hesitated.

Something about this space…it frightened me. My mind conjured images of coiled, black and red vipers, fangs dripping with venom.

Was it a psychic warning? It wasn't like the vision I'd received at Novick City, but it still felt like something was trying to tell me this was dangerous.

And yet—it was the only way forward.

Closing my eyes, I took a slow, steady breath.

Then I lowered myself into the hole.

Chapter: Forty-Six

Weaving my way through the engine room proved to be no problem. The team on duty was battling a small fire that had broken out and filled the space with toxic fumes. It was a fortunate coincidence—but one I welcomed.

From my quick observations, the equipment was ancient and heavily jury-rigged. It was amazing the base was functioning at all. In fact, it was probably one disaster away from complete devastation.

That could work in my favor—if I got desperate enough. But sabotaging this place would be a dangerous gamble. The escape pods likely weren't designed to withstand the nebula, and there were far too many people living aboard. Not everyone would make it out.

Once out of the engine room, I entered a corridor that wasn't crowded like the lower levels. This one was cleaner, brighter, and far better maintained. According to the map M6 was generating in my right-hand periphery, I was in a section of the freighter near the bridge. Up ahead should be a lift running through the vessel's original and added pirate-built levels.

That meant I was only a few levels down from where Sophia had been taken.

Now that I was on board, a few key objectives presented themselves:

- First: determine an escape plan—starting with the bridge.
- Second: locate the Medusa device.

- Third: escape with it—and Sophia—alive.

"There are several people approaching," M6 reported. "Two males, two females."

I pressed myself against the wall as the group neared, laughing and cheering. It became quickly obvious they were drunk and frisky. They couldn't keep their hands off each other, and as they entered the lift, clothing started coming off.

I debated for a moment whether to get in—but judging from their state, this was probably a safe bet. I slipped in just before the door closed.

Noticing that they hadn't pressed any buttons yet, I discreetly pressed the topmost one. No one noticed—everyone was too busy making out.

I pressed myself into the corner as tightly as possible, hoping none of them stumbled into me. Luckily, they didn't. When the lift stopped, none of them looked up to check the floor—too distracted to care.

They were all jolted back to reality when a man with a sawed-off shotgun greeted them with a gruff, "Hello."

The women yanked their tops closed, covering their already exposed chests. The men twisted around, dazed. One of them— probably familiar with the guard—grinned and stumbled toward him with a drunken laugh.

Instead of helping, the guard stepped aside, letting the man fall flat on his face. Everyone burst out laughing—except the guard, who immediately began chastising them.

"What the hell are you thinking? You know this level is restricted!"

One of the other drunk men broke out into another fit of laughter, as though the guard had just told the funniest joke he'd ever heard.

My mind raced, trying to figure out how to get past this guy. But before I could act, the guard raised the shotgun and pointed it at the group.

The man on the floor was helped up by the women, who were no longer amused.

"We're all going to take a little trip back down to where you belong," the guard said. "So stay calm."

With the guard onboard now, the door closed to the lift and I was heading back down again. I wanted to go up, to the bridge.

One of the women piped up, "We must have accidentally pressed the wrong button."

"Hey, it's okay," the guard said with a fake smile. "These things happen. I'm just making sure you all get to the appropriate level. Then you can carry on with your festivities. What were you celebrating?"

"Charlie got that alien device working," the vocal woman said.

Charlie—the laughing man—grinned ear to ear at the mention.

"That's fantastic," the guard said. "The one we took from Zytec? Hopefully, it can be used against—"

Before he could finish, the lift came to a stop. The drunk passengers poured past him into a crowded corridor—and I followed.

Once again, fate had placed me in the right place at the right time. Learning about the Medusa hadn't been my top priority, but if I could find out where it was kept, I'd be foolish to ignore the opportunity. Its location might be known only to a select few.

As I moved with the crowd, a few people bumped into me, but no one paid much attention. The area was packed—definitely a mix of residential and market sectors.

The Voidborn had a functioning economy. A few passing conversations suggested a robust barter system.

My party of drunks finally arrived at a room near the end of the hall. I slipped in with them. The clothes came off almost immediately again, but I ignored the chaos and scanned the apartment.

The lighting was dim—only a pair of weak glow lamps casting a soft moon-like hue. The kitchen was filthy, with pans piled in the sink and trash overflowing. Classic bachelor pad. Two bedrooms—probably shared by the men.

I spotted a scannable badge on the coffee table with a picture of Charlie's grinning face. On the back was a handwritten note:

If found, return to Supervisor Santiago, Workshop Level 6, Section 2.

I searched the apartment a bit longer, taking in small details, then helped myself to a couple of ration bars from the pantry. In a quiet corner, I scarfed one down, trashed the wrapper, and exited.

Weaving my way back through the crowd outside, I kept my eyes open. So far, no other Nomads. Hopefully, the one I'd encountered aboard the freighter had lost my trail.

Someone bumped into me and glanced around—but quickly turned to sell rice grains to a nearby woman.

While I waited for the lift, M6 gave an update.

"Access to the ship's computer is heavily restricted. You'll need to use a spike to retrieve sensitive data or override security."

"I figured. We'll deal with that soon. Right now, I want to check out the workshop. I've got a feeling the Medusa device is being kept there."

"You do realize they could be interrogating Sophia right now," M6 warned.

"She's a big girl. She can handle herself."

"The Voidborn have been known to use inhumane methods to extract information."

"This won't take long," I said, as a lone male entered the lift and selected Level 5.

Once he exited, I selected Level 6.

The corridor was empty. No one in sight.

To my left: a sealed door with a badge scanner labeled Sections 3 and 4. I went right instead. That door read Sections 1 and 2.

I pulled out the badge and scanned it. The door opened with a soft beep.

The workspace beyond was just as empty. Strange—no workers, no noise. Maybe I had arrived during a break or shift change.

I moved forward and let the door close behind me.

The workshop was cluttered with tools, circuit boards, and tangled wires. A busted DIM-series droid lay discarded in the corner, surrounded by what looked like salvaged kitchen appliances.

Metal tables were scattered throughout the room. Toward the back, a set of beaded curtains hung in a doorway.

Pushing through them, I found myself face to face with the Medusa device.

It stood tall, cylindrical, emitting a low thrum. The top half was transparent—and inside it was a woman.

She looked to be in her mid-thirties, with a long scar down the side of her face. As I stared, the scar slowly faded, replaced by fresh skin.

Whatever this thing was doing to her, it wasn't just external— it felt like I was witnessing a miracle of advanced alien engineering.

Leaning in for a closer look, I studied her face.

Her eyes opened—brown orbs locking directly onto mine.

I was phased out…but somehow, I felt like she could *see* me.

Then the device hissed.

The seal broke.

And the barely clothed woman stepped out.

Chapter: Forty-Seven

Even though she was looking straight at me, her hands moved behind her head as she began tying her brunette hair back into a ponytail. She had long legs, a thin torso, and well-developed muscles in her arms.

I was so transfixed that I nearly forgot to step out of her way as she made a beeline for a terminal on a nearby worktable. In my focus on her, I hadn't noticed the red, flashing message on the screen—or the fact that the terminal was linked to the alien device.

I caught a glimpse of strange code running in the background. It looked like some kind of computer language, but definitely not one I recognized.

"Any idea what type of computer language they're running?" I asked.

M6 was silent for a few seconds before replying. "It's not human. That terminal must've come from Zytec as well."

The woman was now reading the message on the screen while pulling a jumpsuit from a nearby chair and slipping it on.

A bald man with burn scars across his face appeared on the terminal.

"Captain, we've got a problem," he said.

Captain? Was *she* the leader of this vessel? Or the entire organization?

"What kind of problem?" she asked, zipping up her jumpsuit.

"The unwanted visitor kind," the bald man said.

Was he referring to me? Sophia? Or something else entirely?

The captain folded her arms across her chest. "Alert the crew to their approach. And remind them not to act out like last time. I don't want a repeat of the disciplinary action taken out on us."

"Understood," the man said before the screen flicked off, leaving only the alien code running in the background.

What the hell had that exchange meant? And *who* was coming that had them so terrified?

The captain lingered in place a few moments, rolling her neck and shoulders before glancing in a mirror on one of the tables. She studied her nearly vanished scar, a small smile curling across her lips.

Then she turned and headed toward the main exit. I followed.

She had her arms crossed again as we rode the lift up to the top floor. The guard who'd escorted the drunks earlier greeted her with a stiff posture and respectful tone.

"Captain," he said. "What should we do? They'll take the device."

She stopped mid-stride and locked eyes with him. "Do nothing," she said, jabbing a finger into his chest. "Understood?"

The guard nodded. She marched past him to the only door straight ahead.

The bridge was a hive of activity. Crew members dashed between consoles, exchanging rapid dialogue. Above us, a transparasteel dome offered a full view of the swirling dark nebula beyond.

"I think I've found a terminal where you can insert the spike," M6 said. "It's along the wall, by the blonde woman."

I wanted to stay close to the captain, but the spike was my only shot at getting critical data—and possibly an escape route.

The blonde was typing rapidly at a console when I approached. I had the spike in hand and quickly spotted a port it would fit. All I needed was a quick distraction.

On the edge of the console sat a tablet in sleep mode. I slid it off the ledge. The woman immediately dove to catch it. As she scrambled to inspect it, I slipped the spike into the port. It began to dissolve into the system.

She didn't even notice.

"This will take some time," M6 said.

I stepped away from the terminal, scanning the room for the captain. She wasn't hard to find—she stood at the center of the bridge, by a large round table displaying a holographic projection of the vessel, the nebula, and an approaching craft.

Moving closer, I had to sidestep several crew members before I found a spot to watch. The approaching vessel was unmistakably an Artran shuttle—those distinctive wing-like protrusions and that long, beak-like nose were impossible to miss.

It was heading toward the forward bow of the pirate base.

What the hell was happening here?

The captain pressed a button on the nearby console and began to speak. Her voice echoed through the ship's speakers.

"Our unwelcome visitors have returned. Everyone is to remain calm and respectful. I do *not* want a repeat of their last visit. If anyone acts out against them, I will personally jettison you out an airlock without remorse. That is all."

She stepped back from the table and turned to the bald man, grabbing his shoulder.

"Let's go greet our guests," she said.

The man stood frozen for a moment, shaking his head. "We should be fighting them."

The captain got right in his face. "Yes, we should. But what happens to the others they took? Are you willing to let them die for our pride? They might be willing to trade all of them for the device we obtained. Now come on. They don't like to be kept waiting."

I followed them back to the lift and down one level to what could only be described as a massive hallway—stretching the entire length of the ship. Hundreds of people lined either side, watching as the captain and the bald man strode between them.

I stayed back near the lift, slipping into a gap in the crowd. The captain was far away, but M6 enhanced my visual feed.

At the end of the corridor, an airlock hissed open.

Three Artrans entered.

They were heavily tattooed with many different symbols—but one stood out among them: a branded human skull on their necks.

That symbol marked them as veterans of the war against humanity.

They moved with their usual awkward, side-to-side gait, their half-cocked legs making them wobble as they walked. They began clicking their tongues—loud, deliberate sounds.

Normally, a translator would be needed—but this time, the words echoed directly in my mind.

"Human filth will serve us," the Artran telepath said.

I didn't know if it was just one speaking…or all three.

Then I felt it: a probing sensation.

Like being underwater, a pressure pushing against my skin—against my mind. I didn't know how to resist. My hand moved on its own, reaching for the alien weapon at my waist.

Then another message, louder this time, roared through my mind:

"There is an imposter among you. A hidden agent. You must kill him."

Every face in the corridor turned.

And they all looked at *me*.

Chapter: Forty-Eight

Reactivating the alien device in my hand—back to its shortened staff form with two glowing energy projectors on either end—I slammed one end into the stomach of a nearby male pirate. Within seconds, his body was propelled backward at an incredible speed, crashing into several others in the hallway.

The impact knocked many of them down, but it didn't stop the horde rushing at me. I was taking hits from every angle, and it didn't matter to them if they struck one of their own.

I saw it happen right in front of me: a male pirate unleashed his shotgun in my direction just as another stepped into the line of fire, trying to raise his rifle. The man dropped without a cry of pain or a flicker of emotion on his face.

The Artrans at the end of the corridor were strong enough telepaths to be controlling these people. If I could take them out, maybe I could stop this madness. But I doubted I'd be welcome aboard after that.

My only real option—for myself, and anyone else left alive—was to find Sophia and get the hell out.

That's why I wasn't using a gun. I didn't want to kill these people. Despite their atrocities and fearsome reputation, they were still human—being manipulated by forces beyond their control.

"M6, what are my options to reach Sophia?" I asked, slamming another pirate in the chest. This one hit the corridor wall with a dull thud and slumped to the floor, unmoving. I didn't think he was dead, but I didn't have time to check.

The deflector shield on my armor blinked red in the lower left of my HUD. I was now taking hits directly to the suit. Bullets pinged off both my front and back plates. I was completely surrounded as I pushed my way toward the elevator.

I knew I could use it to reach Sophia. But then a jolt of pain ripped through my thigh as a bullet cracked the armor plate and tore into the flesh beneath. Another struck my side, and I staggered.

The pain was sharp, but adrenaline pushed me forward. I hit the elevator button and knocked aside another pirate rushing me with a pistol. I slipped inside just as the doors closed, and the lift began rising.

I slumped against the back wall, breathing hard, my heart racing. Flashes of the fight replayed in my mind: a pirate taking aim with a pistol to my left… a shotgun wielder approaching from behind. I had stepped away, and the shotgun blast hit another pirate in the chest instead of me.

Which led me to an important conclusion: the Artrans could sense me, but they couldn't guide their hosts to attack with precision. That was valuable information.

"I still have not gained control of the base systems," M6 reported. "As for exit routes off this ship, there is only one."

"Great. What is it?"

"The elevator shaft is the only route that extends down into the modified cargo containers."

"Are you certain?" I asked.

"There is a seventy-five percent chance there are additional, unidentified routes."

"Understood," I said as the lift opened on Sophia's floor.

The corridor lights were dim and bathed in powerful red strobes. Strangely, no one came at me. The hall was silent. I limped forward, pain increasing with each step. M6 hadn't reported any critical damage, but my body was nearing its limit.

My thigh was stiff, and it hurt to walk. When the door to Sophia's room opened, she was already standing and facing it. I phased in briefly so she'd recognize me.

"What in the hell is happening, Jack?" she asked.

"Artran telepaths," I said. "We have to get out of here. Now."

"What about the Medusa?"

Was she serious? If we didn't leave, we were going to die here.

I grabbed her arm and placed my pistol in her hand. "There's no time. Now follow me."

I stayed phased as we moved back to the lift. I had pulled the hold button earlier to keep the door open. I knew that with the right command override, the lockout could be disabled—but it hadn't been. Not yet.

Which meant one of two things: either the Artrans didn't know who had the override codes, or they couldn't control someone who did. A third option? They *wanted* me to use the lift.

After all, why hadn't they sent pirates through the maintenance shafts to intercept us? M6 had easily identified two alternate access routes to this level.

That thought disturbed me.

The Artrans knew I'd try to escape. They were preparing for it.

I pushed the hold button back in and pressed the lower floor button. But instead of moving, the lights on the console blinked out. The entire lift had been shut down.

"So much for your escape plan," Sophia said.

I looked back at her. "Just means I have to use Plan B."

I pulled her out of the lift and reactivated the alien weapon. This time, instead of twin energy projectors, it formed a single, glowing axe head on one end. I slammed it down into the floor of the lift.

If this was our only path to the lower level, then I'd make my own way through.

After several heavy blows, a decent hole had begun to take shape. But I started coughing—and noticed my hands trembling.

It didn't feel like telepathic influence. Which felt like pressure…like being underwater.

When I looked over at Sophia, she was coughing too. Then she turned and looked toward her room with wide, panicked eyes.

But there was nothing there.

Then she started shooting and screaming.

There was a reason this pirate faction had survived as long as it had—despite their numbers and limited resources.

They used unethical, inhumane warfare tactics.

M6 chimed in: "You have inhaled the Redfall toxin."

I looked at my shaking hand. It stretched unnaturally in front of me, like it had elongated. My vision warped.

Sophia bolted away down the hall.

From her direction came screams—agonized, echoing wails. And then…bootsteps. Heavy. Slow.

Shrouded in mist, a monster approached.

Clad in armor.

Burning orange eyes locked onto me through the haze.

Each bootfall thundered in my audio feed.

I was about to experience the true dread of the Voidborn.

Chapter: Forty-Nine

"There is nothing in front of you, Captain," M6 said over the speaker.

"I see it," I replied, staring down the thing with glowing orange eyes, my axe poised to strike.

"The Voidborn have modified DIM-series droids to deliver holographic projections during battle," M6 said.

"That means they're almost on top of me."

"No, Captain. If that were the case, they wouldn't bother getting this close to you. You need to finish opening the hole in the floor of the lift."

"What about Sophia?" I asked, still hearing the boot steps of the thing. There was something new now—screams echoing in the background. The creature was nearly on top of me, brandishing a bloodstained axe of its own.

Every muscle in my body screamed to run—or at least block the coming strike. Instead, I closed my eyes and let the attack happen.

But no impact came.

When I opened my eyes, the monster had vanished.

In its place stood several more, lurking in the mist—some in front of me, some behind. These ones carried rifles, not axes, and real bullets were suddenly tearing through the air toward me.

"Sophia is lost. Your only chance of survival is to escape," M6 said.

Bullets struck my armor. I felt the stinging impact in my shoulder. M6 was right—I needed to escape. But the gas leaking into my compromised armor was dulling my senses, slowing my reaction time.

It felt like an eternity to swing the alien weapon around the back of my head and drive it down into the breach I had begun cutting in the floor.

I don't know how many more times I was hit before I let the momentum of the axe carry me—headfirst—into the dark shaft.

As I plummeted, I saw what looked like a glowing pit of lava below, bubbling and churning with a hateful orange-red glow. I thought I could see Sophia's face there, just above the surface.

My heart thundered out of control. All I could think about was how painful this death was going to be. I think I screamed. I think someone answered, but their voice was lost in the wind of my fall.

Then, just before impact, I slowed.

I felt the hands of angels gripping my arms. They pulled me upward briefly, then set me free.

My legs hit the ground first. I collapsed into a ball.

I wasn't dead.

There was no lava. No pit of fire.

I was in a cavern.

I could hear the trickle of water echoing through the space, and saw long stalagmites rising from floor and stalactites hanging from the ceiling. Large insects hammered down from above, and I fled deeper into the shadows.

The weapon in my hand brought some comfort—until a beast emerged from the dark, snarling and clawing. I took several hits before swinging the axe deep into its belly, nearly cleaving it in half.

Fresh blood splattered across my visor. I wiped it down to a blurry smear just in time to see more of the creatures swarming me.

I took the head off one. Severed the leg of another. But more came, and with each one, my injuries multiplied.

Past the beasts, I saw them—three demonic figures, all dressed in black. Massive leather wings spread out behind them. Red and orange flames burned from their eyes.

I don't know how, but I knew—they were my tormentors.

The beasts clawed and bit at me as I pushed toward the demons. At last, I reached one and drove my axe through its skull.

Its death sent the creatures into a frenzy.

I was assaulted again, my body now bloody and broken. I collapsed to the ground. I felt teeth sink into my flesh. The pain was overwhelming. No matter how I struggled, I knew what came next.

Death.

But just as one of the beasts' blood-drenched fangs moved for my throat, a female angel with fiery hair appeared. She yanked the creature away and reached out a shimmering white hand toward me.

Barely conscious, I lifted my arm and grasped hers. It was warm. Comforting.

She led me away—to a golden bed with glowing white sheets, where I lay down.

Despite the searing pain in my throat, I managed to speak. "What is this place?"

The angelic being, now joined by several more, circled around the bed. In one voice, they answered:

"Avalon."

Chapter: Fifty

As I lay on the bed, a light of pure white grew brighter and brighter until it completely blocked out the angelic women standing around me. I was alone now, bathed in this all-embracing light. It felt like a warm bath, and all of my injuries, cuts, aches and pains began to ebb away and heal.

I closed my eyes for a moment, still seeing the light behind my lids. When I opened them again, I found myself staring up at a white sun. I was standing now, surrounded by white dunes of sand that stretched endlessly across the horizon.

This place—I had been here before.

Turning in a slow, three-hundred-sixty-degree motion, I spotted black silhouettes of humanoid figures forming around me. The wind blew softly, and I could feel the sand brushing against my face and hands.

I was no longer in my armor, just in the skin-tight black underlay I wore beneath it.

Was this part of the Redfall hallucinogen?

Why did this place feel so real?

A voice boomed in my mind: "Why are you alive?"

Was that a philosophical question?

Looking down at my palms, I realized the time dilation effect of the Redfall toxin had faded. That meant my mental faculties were no longer impaired.

"I don't understand the question," I said.

"Alive, a danger you present," a deeper voice responded in my head.

"A danger to who?" I shot back.

Several voices answered in unison: "To us. To the galaxy."

The last time I had stood in this place, these beings offered to help me prevent another war. They had altered me somehow—I was the one who sent that telepathic burst across the galaxy. And they had done that assuming I wouldn't survive.

Well, I had. And now they didn't know what to do with their mistake.

Using my own voice, I spoke again. "Yes, I lived. I don't know why. Just remove whatever you did to me and let's call it a day."

A deeper voice boomed back: "What was done cannot be undone. We must unmake you to restore balance."

"Unmake me?" I said aloud. "You mean kill me."

Silence.

No response came.

That's when I launched into a verbal assault. If they were going to execute me after everything I'd endured, I wasn't going down quietly.

"If I'm addressing the Ancients—or the Nah-aloy—then everything I've learned about you is wrong. Stories of your great legacy spoke of a powerful race that cherished and preserved life. And now you're passing a death sentence on me—for surviving? Where is that noble, enlightened race I heard stories about? Because it sure as hell isn't standing in this council."

Murmurs filled my head like flies buzzing around my ears—constant, annoying, impossible to swat away.

After several minutes, the same deep voice spoke again in my mind.

"There are powers at work in this galaxy that seek to undermine the foundations of what we left behind. We wish for you to be our agent—to discover what we cannot see."

"I really don't want to serve the interests of others," I said.

"Service is life," a softer, more feminine voice said.

It was an ultimatum. And if I didn't agree…I would likely die. I refused to believe in limited choices, but here I was again—reduced to just one.

Why did I keep playing along?

Why did I want to keep living?

I didn't know why I said it, but the words slipped from my lips: "No."

The finality in that word was staggering. I was sure I'd just signed my own death warrant. Even the murmurs in my mind went silent.

Then came a flash of brilliant light in the sky.

I looked up. The white sun was going supernova again.

This time, when the wave of energy came, I closed my eyes and embraced it. I had accepted my death.

Except—I didn't die.

Instead, my eyes snapped open, and I found myself staring out of a transparent tube.

I was naked, disoriented—but not cold. As my mind began to clear, I realized I was inside the Medusa device.

Standing nearby was the brunette-haired captain I had observed earlier.

Why was I in here?

Why was I still alive?

The seal of the device hissed open, and I instinctively lifted myself to get a better look around the room. A paranoid fear gripped me—armed guards standing by, ready to finish me off.

But there were none.

The woman stepped back, keeping her hands at her sides.

"Why?" was the first word out of my mouth.

Her eyes met mine, and she raised a single eyebrow.

"I was going to ask you the same question," she said.

Chapter: Fifty-One

"Who placed me in this device?" I asked. I wasn't sure that should've been my first question. After all, my recent memories were strange and disturbing. Unless I believed an angel had placed me inside this device, I needed answers.

"I did," she said.

If that was true, then how had she resisted the Artran telepaths?

I nodded slowly. "How did you resist the Artrans?"

The response came quick and sharp. "I didn't."

"Did they tell you to keep me alive?"

"No. They wanted you dead," she said. "And in response to any of your other questions: no, I'm not under their control anymore—and I want to know why."

"What makes you think I had anything to do with that?"

She crossed her arms over her chest. "Because they were terrified of you. I could feel the hatred as they used my body to assault you."

"That still doesn't explain anything. So...what happened to the Artrans?"

A grin cracked across her face. "You killed them."

She said it so matter-of-factly. I had no recollection of killing anyone in my hallucinogenic state. Just vague images of beasts, angels, and demons.

"How exactly did I kill them?"

"That's the most interesting part," she said. "You killed them with your mind. So what are you?"

"I'm a man," I replied, unsure how to defend myself against questions I didn't fully understand.

"Are you a product of Zytec?" she asked.

"You have to be," she muttered. "Why else would you have come with Sophia? They sent you to recover this device."

I shook my head. "It's not what you think."

"Then explain," she snapped.

"Everyone at Zytec is dead," I said. "I came here with Sophia to recover the device—but for our own reasons. Zytec made us dependent on a drug we have to take every few days."

She nodded, pacing now. "I'm aware of that. But the fact that you needed the drug implies you were part of Zytec."

"I wasn't," I said, raising my voice. "I was manipulated. Forced into service. I was only trying to break free—and so was Sophia."

She gave a short, humorless chuckle. "I don't think you know your traveling companion very well."

She was right. I didn't know Sophia well. And if what I feared about her was true, a cold chill ran up my spine. The layers of deception could be deeper than I thought.

"You're right. So, I'll speak only for myself. Here's the truth."

"At last," she said. "I can't wait to hear it."

"Even though I don't look like it, I'm Jack Donovan. Zytec saved my life, altered my face and DNA, and planned to use me as a ghost operative."

"What about your abilities?" she asked.

"They started to develop after I was exposed to an alien device we code-named the Omega Mirror."

Her gaze dropped to the floor, and she resumed pacing. Several minutes passed before she spoke again.

"If you're the Jack Donovan who's been in the news, and you have that kind of power...then why sneak around my vessel? Why not just take it?"

A good question. And I only had one answer.

"Because I have no idea how to use my abilities. Or their range. Or their strength. If I did kill those Artrans... I don't know how I did it."

She stopped pacing and locked eyes with me. "That story is strange enough that I actually believe most of it. Put your clothes on."

"I've told you the truth," I said.

"I have no desire to repeat myself," she said flatly. "I saved your life. Now I need you to help save mine—and thousands of others."

With that, she stepped through the beaded curtain and out of the room, leaving me to consider her words.

If the Artran telepaths were dead, and they didn't return to their base soon, then a larger force might be sent to investigate. And if they found their comrades dead, everyone aboard this vessel might die.

And it would be my fault.

Lifting myself out of the Medusa device, I found my underlay garment crumpled on the floor—bloody and shredded. It was useless now. I searched for anything wearable.

On one of the nearby worktables was a gray jumpsuit, neatly folded. I slid into it, glancing around for my armor—or what remained of it. No luck.

The woman returned with a pair of flip-flops in hand.

They looked too small, but she tossed them at my feet. "Put those on," she said.

As expected, my toes stuck out over the front, and I couldn't stand the strap between them. I would've preferred going barefoot.

"I've given you my name," I said. "What's yours?"

"You can call me Captain—for now," she replied. "Now let's take a walk."

I wiggled my toes inside the sandals, still uncomfortable, then looked back at her. She was half-turned, holding the curtain aside.

"Okay, Captain. Let's take a walk."

We were in the lower levels of the ship. I'd been here before—it wasn't heavily populated. We stepped onto the lift, now repaired with a fresh bottom plate covering the hole I had made.

"How long was I in the Medusa?" I asked.

"A couple of hours," she replied, pressing the top button.

"So...when did you become leader of the Voidborn? Last intel I had said a man named Dante was in charge."

That was a lie. I knew Dante was dead—killed by the Nomad named Colbosh, the one Admiral Frost had been hunting since Novick City. I just wanted to see how truthful she would be.

"Dante was a monster," she said. "Under his leadership, we saw more bloodshed and cruelty than you can imagine. You won't find anyone here shedding a tear for that man."

"And yet...there are still kidnappings, rapes, and torture happening at nearby colonies."

She gave me a hard look, those brown eyes drilling into me. "Those are remnants of Dante's followers—people who thrive on death and chaos. I've been trying to bring peace. I want the Voidborn to return to the fold of the Colonial Earth Forces."

She looked away, her expression distant. Something haunted her.

"When did the Artrans find your base?" I asked.

Her tone softened. "Two or three weeks after I was voted in. Since then, we've lived in constant fear. They can torture us...force us to act against our will. We've tried hiding, but they keep finding us— and punishing us."

Had the Artrans decoded Voidborn navigation? Or was it part of their expanding telepathic power?

She continued. "Worse, they took many of us. They're enslaved somewhere."

"You think they have a base in the nebula?"

"We suspected it. Now we know. Thanks to the vessel still docked. My techs are going over every inch of it."

"So what's your plan?"

The lift paused on a mid-level. Outside, sheets covered bloodstained bodies. Women and children sobbed and moved about the corridor. A woman who had called the lift looked at me, fists clenched, teeth bared.

If the Captain hadn't intervened, she would've attacked me.

When the door closed again, I looked her in the eye. "All those bodies...was that my doing?"

"It was," she said, nodding. "Now I see why Zytec wanted you."

I hadn't meant to kill anyone. "I'm sorry," I muttered, unable to meet her eyes.

Could I have done something differently? Maybe if I had reached the Artrans sooner, this bloodshed could've been avoided.

She moved closer and shoved me against the lift wall.

"The real blame is on the Artrans. They caused this. They used us. They escalated this conflict. And we paid in blood. If you feel remorse—like I do—then help us end this."

"What must I do?"

She stepped back.

"I have a plan," she said.

Chapter: Fifty-Two

The plan was simple: fly the Artran vessel back to its base, unleash a dozen veteran soldiers onboard, recover the hostages, and kill as many Artran as possible along the way.

There was only one glaring flaw. The captain was counting on me to somehow counter or kill the Artran telepaths. A nice idea in theory—except I had no conscious control over how I'd done it before, or even if I really had.

"Any ideas yet, M6?" I asked aloud from inside my helmet.

The technicians had patched my armor together with Voidborn parts. I couldn't phase anymore, and the deflector was permanently destroyed. In essence, I was wearing little more than enhanced body armor now—except M6 was still rooted into the system.

"I have several suggestions based on my research," M6 replied, "but none can be tested without direct confrontation with the Artran."

"That's going to happen very soon. So go ahead. Because I haven't come up with a single decent idea."

"Some metaphysical literature suggests that telepathic ability is closely tied to emotional states and the images one can control in their mind."

"Not helpful," I muttered. "I'm not going to be thinking peaceful thoughts while someone's trying to kill me."

"You don't need peace of mind," M6 said. "You can be angry. But the first method is to mentally visualize a barrier—an energy bubble. If you can hold the image, you may be able to block the Artran from locating you psychically."

"What about the soldiers? How do I keep them from being turned against me?"

"The same principle applies. If your mental shield proves effective, you may be able to expand it to encompass others— shielding them as well."

"That's going to take serious concentration. What else do you have?"

"Another possible method: counterattack. Flood your mind with violent, angry thoughts. Create a psychic storm. Several historical accounts reference this tactic as well."

"At least I've got something to try. Now patch me into the main intercom."

"The mic is open, Captain," M6 said.

I addressed the soldiers seated in the bay behind me. "We're entering the atmosphere. Get ready for touchdown."

The nav data found aboard the Artran ship indicated they were operating out of a facility on a planet deep inside the nebula. The surface was dead—no life, no vegetation—but as I approached the coordinates, a massive volcano rose into view. Carved into the side of it was a wide opening—just big enough for two vessels to pass through.

A shimmering forcefield covered the entrance, and I was closing in fast.

"The Artran are trying to communicate," M6 reported.

"Let them hear static," I said. "And power up the missile."

Voidborn techs had retrofitted the Artran ship with a high-yield missile beneath the hull. The plan was simple: blow our way into the base. There was no chance they'd open the door for us.

"We're at optimal range," M6 confirmed.

"Fire."

The missile launched at high velocity and impacted the forcefield in seconds. A brilliant explosion shattered a portion of the shield around the entrance, throwing up a dense dust cloud.

M6 immediately interfaced with the ship's systems, projecting a virtual holographic overlay of what lay ahead.

Even though the Artran were considered an elder race by our scientists, their tech wasn't leagues beyond ours. In fact, before the war, they had bought weapons, ships, and ammunition from us. That was why M6 had no trouble integrating with their systems—this ship was powered by human-made tech.

"M6, what am I looking at?"

Through the dust cloud, I could see that a large portion of the volcano had blown away—revealing something unnatural beneath the rock: clean, geometric surfaces, artificial. The forcefield around the ship entrance was down, but strangely, the area itself looked untouched.

"What the hell is that made of?" I asked.

"This is an artificial construct," M6 said. "I have no further data beyond current scans."

"How old is it?" I asked, thinking back to when the Golar Nebula formed.

"There is debate, but a reasonable estimate places the supernova events that created the nebula at around thirty thousand years ago."

I let out a low whistle. This place had probably been built by the Ancients—or at least by some other advanced civilization lost to time.

But I didn't have time to contemplate ancient architecture. I brought the ship down into the opening and landed hard, lowering the rear ramp.

The Voidborn soldiers moved fast—deploying mist canisters and releasing their swarm of DIM-series droids, which began projecting combat holograms throughout the bay.

Then it hit me.

That familiar underwater pressure—pushing at the edges of my consciousness.

The Artran were probing.

I tried the mental barrier technique M6 suggested. I imagined a bubble of energy enveloping me.

The pressure vanished instantly.

I paused, mentally prodding myself to be sure it wasn't just a fluke. It was gone. The probe had stopped.

Outside the cockpit window, I could see and hear rifle fire erupting in the misty bay. M6 patched into the squad's comms—and confirmed my worst fear.

The Artran telepaths were taking control of the soldiers.

Knowing that my barrier had worked, I tried expanding it—enveloping the bay, the soldiers, the ship.

At first, it was easy. I could imagine it working.

But then I looked outside.

Several Voidborn stood near the ship, rifles in hand, staring up at me.

And I realized just how wrong I had been.

Before I could even turn in the pilot's chair, bullets tore through the cockpit.

I was left with no choice but to fight back—against the very soldiers I had brought to this place.

Chapter: Fifty-Three

Spinning to the left in the pilot's chair, I hurled the alien device straight at the single pirate soldier blocking the door. The device, still downsized and glowing bright purple at one end, twisted through the air like a thrown axe.

My rifle was already raised and aimed. I squeezed the trigger at the same moment the device struck the soldier. I wasn't sure what would happen—but I was surprised when the impact sent him flying backward with the force of a shockwave.

It cleared the way.

I advanced, retrieving the alien device at the door's edge and moving forward. Two soldiers lay crumpled at the bottom of the ramp—one unmoving, the other on hands and knees, struggling to stand.

Instead of shooting immediately, I tried the mental bubble again—this time on a smaller scale. I paused, picturing the protective field surrounding just myself and the nearby soldier.

He stood, shaking his head, then looked up at me—then down at his fallen comrade. When he looked back, he tapped his helmet.

"M6, do you have a direct link to that soldier?"

"You are patched in now, Captain."

"Listen carefully," I said. "The Artran have taken control of your team. I can disrupt their influence, but I have to be close."

The soldier gave a nod, raised his rifle, and began scanning the misty bay with military focus.

"Let's move forward, slowly," I said, expanding the bubble in my mind, just a bit further, praying I hadn't reached the limit of its range.

As we reached the ramp's bottom, two more soldiers flanked us from either side. I took several rounds to the chest, grunting as I staggered. I shouted for the other soldier to fall back inside the ship.

He laid down suppressing fire as he retreated, but took a few hits of his own and stumbled backward. Then both attackers rushed the ramp—but as they reached the top, they froze, rifles raised, eyes uncertain.

"I've added them to your open channel," M6 said.

"Stay close to us at all costs," I instructed, fighting to maintain the mental barrier. This concentration during combat wouldn't hold forever—and I still had no idea how far I could extend it.

"I can keep us safe from Artran control—but only at short range."

None of them responded verbally. Instead, I saw a flurry of hand signals between them.

"M6, can you translate?"

"Some of it matches American Sign Language, but there are deviations—battlefield variants. I'll record and analyze it later."

"Do that. Now, what do we know about the layout of this place?"

"The DIM droids are mapping the bay in real time. Not all soldiers have been compromised."

"Show me."

My visor lit up with a tactical map. M6 outlined the bay—three lines of parked ships, with blue and red dots marking friendly and enemy forces. The blue ones were ours. The reds, Artran-controlled. A few blue dots were inside our vessel.

So, the red dots—about a dozen—were toward the back of the bay near a door. I doubted all were telepaths.

"Group of four on the right side is fending off five Voidborn soldiers under telepathic control," M6 added.

"Mark them yellow," I said. "Send this to the squad. We move out."

The image of the bubble faltered for a moment as I shifted focus. "What about the hostages?"

"No intel yet."

I was already moving toward the embattled yellow group. "We're intercepting the yellow squad. Stick close, stay quiet. These Artran telepaths aren't as strong as the ones who attacked your base, but we're not out of danger. Move fast—we still have time to save the hostages."

A new flurry of hand signals passed between the soldiers. They formed a loose perimeter around me as we pushed into the mist. The firefight sounds ahead were close now. The DIM droids updated the map.

Eight red dots were now flanking around to our rear. Four remained huddled near the exit.

"Change of plans," I said. "Head straight for the four by the exit."

More hand signals followed. I increased our pace. Rifle fire erupted through the haze. I could feel the presence of telepaths nearby—the psychic pressure like deep water pushing in on me.

I pushed back with the bubble.

We stepped over fallen Artran soldiers as we advanced. The mist was thinning, and I caught sight of the four robed figures near the bay exit.

A shot rang out—one of the Voidborn scored a headshot. The bullet burst a greenish mass across the others. The remaining three fled. I felt the psychic pressure vanish almost instantly.

But the threat wasn't gone.

The Artran-controlled soldiers from earlier were sweeping around to hit us from behind. We ducked behind one of the parked ships for cover.

My visor updated. The newly freed Voidborn were moving in, engaging the Artran from the opposite side. The blue dots were up to nine—three had died during the conflict.

One nearby soldier tapped me and motioned for me to follow—but as I stood—

—my mind blanked.

I was suddenly standing in a cavernous room with a tall, pitch-black obelisk stretching from floor to ceiling. Six Artran in black robes circled it, unmoving, staring at its surface.

The air was frigid. The stink of sulfur hung thick.

As I stepped closer, I could feel energy radiating from the obelisk. The hairs on my arms stood up.

Then I looked into it.

Something ancient, something hateful, looked back.

I should have turned away—but instead, I leaned in.

"You will not hide your secrets from me," I said, not even sure why.

Suddenly, one of the robed Artran lunged, tackling me. I hit the ground hard. It straddled me, and I was transfixed by the black voids in its eyes—bottomless, dead.

Then it vanished.

I was back in reality, looking into the visor of a Voidborn soldier.

What the hell had I just seen?

Why did I feel this overwhelming pull, this compulsion to go deeper into the base?

I sat down next to the ship, breathing heavily, trying to shake the obsession. Minutes passed before I could stand again and re-establish the mental barrier.

This had been too easy so far. The stronger telepaths hadn't even shown themselves yet.

Gunfire erupted from behind the ship.

Peering through the haze, I spotted it.

Dead Artran soldiers—shambling forward.

Just like at the embassy.

They were using it again.

I should have expected this. I'd seen it on Mars.

Now they were behind us.

Cutting off our escape route.

I had been a fool.

Chapter: Fifty-Four

I watched as the soldiers around me riddled the bodies with more bullets, but it didn't slow their advance. In fact, it only sent the dead into a frenzy. They began running toward us in an awkward, out-of-control charge.

My rifle was nearby, but after seeing bullets have no effect, I reached for the alien device and activated it. Once again, I configured it into a shortened staff, energy blades extending from both ends.

There was no point in trying to spare the undead. I needed to understand how the Artran were capable of this. It just didn't seem possible.

M6 spoke as I engaged my first target. One of the reanimated had run straight into the end of my weapon and was now struggling to reach me with flailing arms and snapping teeth.

"I have completed an analysis of our current situation," M6 said.

"I'm listening," I replied, stepping back and yanking the blade out of the thing's chest. It lunged forward instantly, but I was ready. I spun the staff in an arc and cleaved through its head, the upper half severed cleanly.

The body collapsed, twitching.

"In theory," M6 continued, "Artran telepaths can control newly deceased victims due to residual neurochemical activity in the brain. This doesn't decay immediately and could allow control for up to an hour post-mortem."

"That's good to know, M6. But what I need is a way to stop them."

Before I could engage another Artran, a fully armored Voidborn soldier charged me from the rear of the vessel. He had slipped past the others and tried to bull-rush me.

I caught just enough of a glimpse to pivot and dodge—just as another undead Artran leapt at me from the side.

Falling back to gain space, I was now facing attackers from two sides—until a third reanimated Artran dropped on me from above.

They were targeting me specifically. The Artran controllers wanted me dead.

"M6, do you have an update on what's beyond that door?" I asked, sweeping low with the staff and severing an Artran's leg.

"Not yet. One of the DIM droids reports complications decoding the locking mechanism. A Voidborn is planting explosives, but odds of breaching are estimated at twenty-five percent."

The undead Voidborn charged again. I aimed high at the helmet but missed. Twisting around to avoid being tackled, I slashed across its back. The blades dug deep into the armor and dropped it to its knees.

Seizing the opportunity, I moved to strike at the neck.

That's when another undead Artran landed on top of me.

The impact was brutal, knocking me flat. I was dazed. The thing on top of me began prying at my helmet, trying to get to my face.

My alien weapon had been knocked from my grip. I wasn't sure where it had landed. I reached for my pistol, just as I felt the helmet begin to lift off.

Fingers clawed into my neck. Pain. Blood.

I panicked and fired blindly.

The pressure didn't stop. I couldn't breathe. I emptied the entire clip into the thing before a Voidborn soldier kicked it off me and shot it point-blank in the head.

The soldier extended a hand. I took it, adjusting my helmet back into place.

"You've sustained minor scratches and bruising to the larynx," M6 reported.

Back on my feet, the soldier handed the alien device back to me before turning to engage another undead attacker.

"I'm fine, by the way," I muttered.

"Noted. I have also updated the map. The locked door opened just a few seconds ago."

Why would the Artran do that? They could have reinforced their position and overwhelmed us. Now they were inviting us in?

Their tactics didn't make sense.

"How many hostiles are left in the bay?" I asked, reactivating the alien device.

"None," M6 replied. "However, you did lose one more soldier to the undead."

I didn't have time to grieve. I didn't know these people—but I understood tactics. And right now, the enemy was wearing us down. Reducing our numbers. Draining our resources.

We should've pulled out—but I doubted the others would agree. It was possible many had loved ones among the hostages.

And who was I to deny them a chance to save them?

Even if it cost us our lives.

One of the Voidborn soldiers tapped my shoulder and motioned for me to follow. Once again, I was surrounded as we advanced through the open door.

And once again, I reforged the bubble in my mind.

Chapter: Fifty-Five

The corridor beyond the bay was definitely alien in design. It was opal-shaped, narrowing toward the top, and the material of the walls shimmered like living water beneath an obsidian mirror.

Any light that shone into it produced swirling patterns of dark color, which evaporated quickly once you stopped looking. The passage was wide enough for the entire team to stay circled around me.

But all of us felt a growing sense of confusion the farther we traveled inward. At times, it felt like we were walking uphill, even though the ground appeared flat. At other moments, it seemed like we were being forced to curve around a bend that didn't physically exist.

It was disorienting—and it made my stomach churn.

What disturbed me even more was the faint chiming sound I kept hearing, like an old wind chime swaying lazily on someone's porch in the summer.

M6 couldn't confirm any auditory hallucinations. And the strangest part: it felt like we'd been walking for at least ten minutes, but when I glanced back, the door to the bay was still visible.

Was this place bending the laws of time and space? Or just playing mind games with us?

The recent vision of the obelisk had left me shaken. I knew—intellectually—that we were dealing with ancient, powerful technology. The real question was: left behind by *who*? And for *what purpose*?

After another minute of walking, we reached a dead end. When I turned to look behind us, the corridor stretched endlessly into black.

"Any suggestions?" I asked M6.

"It is possible that the creators of this place designed it as a test of some kind," M6 replied.

"Or a very elaborate security system," I said. "In my vision, there was a chamber with an obelisk in the center. Robed Artran were standing around it, staring into it. I got the sense it functioned like the Omega Mirror."

"Why were the Artran wearing black robes?" M6 asked. "That contradicts their cultural beliefs—specifically their tradition of avoiding clothing."

"Not sure. Maybe the robes were metaphorical."

"That is highly likely," M6 said. "If the obelisk functions similarly to the Omega Mirror, it supports my theory that this place is a testing ground for adepts."

"So, what should I do?"

"Why not focus your thoughts on what you want from this place—and observe what happens?"

It was a good idea.

I moved through the circle of Voidborn and stepped close to the obsidian wall, placing my gloved hand against it. The surface was solid, cold, and metallic—yet as I touched it, red swirls began to form beneath my palm.

I thought of the obelisk chamber. Nothing happened.

Then I closed my eyes and visualized the scene in detail—every feature, every shadow, every robed figure.

Even before I opened my eyes, I sensed something had shifted.

Through the helmet's enhanced audio, I could hear shouting. Voices barking commands. Explosions in the distance. And a smell—burning circuits and melted wiring—seeped through my compromised armor.

What was I experiencing? Why couldn't I *see* any of this?

My eyes were open—but there was only blackness.

Then one familiar voice brought everything into focus.

Admiral Thadd.

"Concentrate your fire on those bombers! We must protect Earth at all costs!"

It was like a switch flipped. Suddenly, I was standing on the bridge of Thadd's flagship, watching him command from the central console as a holographic display of Earth flickered before him. Around it, a swarm of CEF ships clashed with the overwhelming Artran fleet.

I could move—walk—breathe. This wasn't just a vision. I was there.

The bridge was in chaos. Several consoles along the walls had exploded. Crewmen fought fires. Burned bodies lay where they fell.

"M6, are you seeing this? Am I really here?"

No response.

If this was a telepathic projection…it felt too real. The smells. The heat. The sound of sparking wires and distant rumbling. I had never been on this bridge. This wasn't a memory.

And I doubted the Artran had been present to witness this moment.

I stepped closer to Thadd. His white uniform was stained with soot. Blood streaked his sleeves. Part of his face had been burned. But he stood resolute, leaning over the console, watching his outnumbered fleet struggle to hold the line while Earth was being bombed.

I had read the classified reports. Thadd had even told me his story firsthand. But nothing compared to this.

The grim look on his face. The fury in his voice as he pounded his fist on the console, barking orders and pointing at enemy ships. He was commanding while his world fell apart around him.

In frustration, I called out, "Why am I here? What's the point of this?"

Crackling static filled my helmet's speaker—then a voice.

M6…or something that *sounded* like him. Colder. Sharper.

"You have a choice to make."

"A choice? This event already happened. Time *can't* be changed."

Silence.

Could I really be here, in this moment, at this time and place?

And if so…what could I *do*?

I looked past the holographic table and out the forward transparasteel window. Earth burned below us. Cities crumbling. Fire blooming across continents.

What if I could change this?

What if I could save my wife and daughter?

I didn't need to convince myself any further.

If I had the power to stop this—then I would.

I clenched my fists, fingernails biting into my palms.

Images of destruction. Dead families. Burned-out homes. All of it filled my mind. I funneled that rage into the Artran fleet—imagining their ships exploding, their commanders screaming, their forces dying in waves.

I was going to kill every last one of them.

Chapter: Fifty-Six

In my rage, I had moved past the bridge crew and stations and was now standing directly against the transparasteel window, focusing intently on the Artran warships bombarding Earth.

Despite the intense images of death and destruction I projected at the enemy, no ships exploded. The bombardment didn't stop. Maybe I just wasn't strong enough. Maybe it had all been a fool's hope—a desperate chance to rewrite history.

An image of my wife and daughter's crushed bodies filled my mind. I didn't want to see it. I didn't want to confront it. Their cold, lifeless forms—intertwined in a final, desperate attempt at protection—lay before me. I could have saved them.

Hot tears streaked down my cheeks.

I will save them.

At some point in my silent fury, I let out a primal scream—one I imagined should've shattered the fragile glass in front of me.

Instead, what came was a sudden cessation of hostilities. As if the Artran had heard me—or felt my intent to destroy them.

"They're retreating!" someone shouted behind me.

I didn't turn. I wanted visual confirmation. Pressing my face closer to the cool glass, I saw the wing-shaped Artran warships veering off—fleeing into jump space.

"Why did they retreat?" another voice asked.

Followed by: "What the hell just happened?"

Then Thadd's voice: "We'll figure that out later. Get those fires out!"

I stood transfixed, staring at Earth. The damage had been done. But something was dawning on me—maybe I had been the catalyst. Maybe I had stopped the Artran bombardment.

Was it possible?

Then the voice—not quite M6—came back over my helmet.

"Worthy."

"Worthy of what?" I asked, as the bridge began to fade.

This had been a test. One with real consequences. I now stood again in the black void—until the chamber with the obelisk coalesced around me.

Though it looked like a cavern buried deep underground—stalagmites rising from the floor—there was a strange warmth emanating from the obelisk.

At its base, where I had once seen black-robed Artran standing and gazing into it, now lay their bodies—crumpled and decaying. The stench was unbearable. Some had clearly been dead for days.

"M6, are you there?"

A crackle preceded the reply. "I have a temporary time loss in my memory."

"It's okay," I said. "I'll explain everything once we get out of here."

"That may not be possible. This cavern is self-contained. I detect no entrance or exit. It's as if we are sealed in a bubble beneath the surface."

"I think this thing was testing me. Testing how powerful a telepath I've become."

"And what conclusion have you arrived at?"

"I think I was able to alter history somehow."

"If that's true," M6 replied, "then what the beings from the Omega Mirror did to you is beyond the realm of known science."

I walked slowly toward the obelisk, my eyes drawn to its shimmering obsidian surface. As I neared, I noticed something peculiar: the reflection in the surface showed only me—no cavern, no bodies. Just me.

In my earlier vision, I had sensed hatred emanating from it. But now…now it felt like a welcome. Like I was an honored guest. I could feel it pulling me in—beckoning me to touch its surface and look deeper.

"Are you sure you should do this, Captain?" M6 asked.

"I don't think I have much of a choice—not if I want to get us out of here alive."

I reached out—and touched it.

***

The cavern dimmed. Not in darkness, but as if I were seeing everything through a pane of obsidian glass. My hand jerked back reflexively. I took a step away, trying to understand what had just happened.

Then I noticed it—standing to my right, beside the obelisk.

An alien.

Humanoid. Dark gray skin. Pointed ears. Bald. Solid silver eyes. Its black robes were adorned with intricate, arcane symbols.

"Who are you?" I asked, unsure if that was the right question.

The being blinked slowly. Then a voice—human in tone—spoke *directly* into my mind.

"The best description, in your language, would be…judgment."

"Okay… I passed your first test—otherwise I wouldn't be here. So, what do you want from me?"

"Help," the alien said. "The bodies you see were not strong enough. But you…you possess a power far greater than we believed possible for such a young race."

I didn't know how to respond. If it could read my mind, then surely it knew about the Omega Mirror and the council of beings that had awakened this ability in me.

"It doesn't matter how you came by your abilities," the voice said. "What matters is your willingness to help. After all, I showed you a glimpse of the raw, unrefined power you now possess."

I hesitated. "Can you explain what just happened? That test—did I really affect the outcome?"

"Of course. Though placed into a past event telepathically, you were initially only meant to observe. But powerful telepaths can cause ripples in time. Wakes, as you call them."

"So, it was me. I caused the Artran retreat."

"You did more than that, Jack Donovan. Your psychic wake terrified them. They believed a human telepath was about to destroy their entire fleet."

If I'd only acted sooner, I thought. *I could've saved my wife and daughter. Why was I so slow? So blind?*

"You have a disciplined mind," the alien said, "but this tragedy still grips you. To reach full mastery, you must let it go—or it will destroy everything around you."

"But those emotions—they were what fueled me during the test. How can they be a bad thing?"

"You'll have to take my word. If we had more time, I could show you."

"Why don't we have time? This place has been here for thousands of years."

The alien nodded. "It has. But what the Artran started—what they failed to complete—is now collapsing. If it closes, it cannot be reopened."

"You're not explaining. *What's* closing?"

"You already suspect the answer," it said. "Yes. The Artran were trying to open a portal—to my side of the universe."

"And if I open that portal?" I asked, picturing a rift in space filled with warships. If the Nah-aloy had struggled to stop them, humanity had no chance.

"I see the vision in your mind," it said.

I was getting tired of it reading my thoughts. Maybe the mental bubble would still work here. I focused—and felt the shield snap into place.

"You only know half the story," it continued—now forced to speak aloud. "The Nah-aloy invaded *our* space. They were the ones who tried to enslave us with telepathic domination. We were not aggressors. We were victims."

With the bubble up, I studied its body language carefully. No obvious tells of deceit—but I still had questions.

"Why come here? Why not stay where you are?"

There was no hesitation.

"We are few. We seek sanctuary. The Nah-aloy turned the other races against us."

M6 said nothing. Which either meant he didn't function here—or this was all in my head.

I knew almost nothing about the ancient war between the Nahaloy and the Opeciens. Could this being be telling the truth?

"Jack," the alien said, "I know this is confusing. I wish I had more time. But I am begging you—this is our only hope."

Its tone didn't change. The words were emotionless. Maybe it couldn't express feeling.

I glanced around. The bodies of the Artran who had tried to commune with the obelisk lay where they had fallen.

If I help…what guarantees do I have that you'll let me go?

"Look behind you, Jack."

I turned. A shimmering portal had opened—revealing the hallway. The Voidborn stood just beyond, pointing toward me. They could see me—but couldn't reach me.

A do-or-die moment.

I hated making decisions without enough information. And my instincts screamed not to trust this being.

But if I'm as powerful as it claims…then why can't I get the answers I need?

Maybe intention was the key.

Focusing on the being, I dropped the bubble—and replaced it with a single, crystal-clear command in my mind:

Truth.

Chapter: Fifty-Seven

The neutral expression on the alien's face dropped into a frown. It lowered its chin and widened its silver eyes at me.

"I beg you for help in good faith, Jack—and you dare turn your feeble skills against me?" the alien said in a lowered voice.

There was no turning back now.

"I don't trust you," I said, standing my ground.

"One last chance, Jack. Please…help us."

I swear I saw a swirl of dark blue ripple through those bright silver eyes.

"If you kill me," I said, "you'll never get my help opening the rift. So why are you so afraid to let me see the truth?"

"Truth is a subjective perspective," it said. "If you glimpse something without context, that 'truth' becomes whatever your mind imagines."

I wasn't sure how the being was blocking me, but I could feel that same strange sensation again—like water pressure against my skin. It made me wonder if I was dealing with a physical entity.

Doubling down, I closed my eyes. My fists clenched instinctively as I fully visualized the alien in my mind and took a step forward. I intended to dig the information out of its thoughts.

Instead of reacting with aggression, the alien calmly clasped its hands behind its back.

I rushed forward and struck out.

But my fist didn't hit flesh—it struck a swirling wall of light. I staggered back.

"You have no idea how this works," the alien's voice echoed in my mind. "Let me show you."

An invisible force slammed into me, knocking me to the ground. Everything went black for a second.

When I came to, I was back in the cavern—but it had changed. A bluish light now pulsed and swirled within the obelisk. The alien stood watching me.

"I had hoped you would help us willingly, Jack. But I see now...you need more convincing."

A searing pressure built in my skull. Like something was trying to force its way out. I screamed and tried to focus—tried to rebuild the bubble in my mind to block the assault.

But before I could form it, everything blanked out again.

Now I was kneeling in a pool of acid.

It burned my hands and face. The air reeked of sulfur, and distant screams echoed all around me.

I managed a glance—others were in the acid too, their bodies writhing in agony. Lava flowed from cracks in the ceiling. Giant figures roamed the hellscape, cracking whips over the suffering.

"It's fascinating," the alien said. "This concept of the afterlife, born from your mind."

It stepped aside, revealing my wife and daughter—screaming and pleading in the acid.

"No!" I choked.

Mentally, I knew this wasn't real. But the pain was. My skin felt like it was melting from my bones.

The alien had the upper hand—more skilled, more practiced. But I had the power. It said so itself. It needed me.

Eyes closed, I focused on each breath. I pushed out the fear. The pain. The screams.

I rebuilt the bubble in my mind.

I felt the blows against it—like sledgehammers pounding my thoughts—but I held steady. Centered.

Then I opened my eyes.

Now it was the alien whose eyes were closed, head bowed in concentration. The cavern had changed again—now displaying a sweeping panorama of images.

Behind the alien, massive warships emerged from a rift in space. To the left, entire worlds burned. Alien forces enslaved entire populations.

As I circled around, the visions blended—my past, the present, and a grim future where these beings dominated every corner of our galaxy.

"I refuse your offer," I said firmly.

The alien's eyes opened. Blue veins bulged beneath the skin around them.

"Then you will die here," it said weakly.

The images vanished, and the cavern returned. The floor and ceiling shook as rocks rained down.

"Death and I are old friends," I said. "I'm prepared. Are you?"

The pounding resumed against my bubble. I felt the force of it against my skin, especially near my chest. One strike knocked the wind from my lungs.

The sudden disruption broke my focus.

Then—blackness again.

I was submerged in thick, warm liquid. Black and suffocating. It squeezed my body, dragging me downward.

Instinctively, I reached up. Above me, a rift shimmered—just barely large enough to wedge a few fingers through.

Desperation surged. I put everything into prying it open. The weight of the liquid grew heavier. I widened the opening—enough to force my head through, then my shoulders. I fought like hell.

Then I realized:

I had been tricked.

Fooled into doing exactly what the alien wanted.

The damage was done.

Was it too late?

I gave in. Let the black liquid pull me under.

If I could just refocus—rebuild the bubble—I might be able to stop whatever was happening.

But I panicked.

I couldn't breathe.

I couldn't move.

The black liquid filled my lungs.

And then—

Darkness.

Chapter: Fifty-Eight

Pain and desperation—that's all I could remember of my death. It wasn't until I was staring into the bright orange eyes of a demon that I realized I was alive again. Death had been cheated of its prize once more.

My body instinctively tried to curl into a defensive ball, recoiling from the perceived terror—except my limbs didn't respond. Everything felt weak and hollow. My mental state was no better. It took me far too long to recognize the demon's face for what it really was: a Voidborn soldier.

Somehow, they had saved me.

At first, they tried to help me to my feet, but when that failed, I was strapped to one of their backs and carried piggyback-style.

I couldn't focus on any one thing as we moved back into the bay. The soldiers were firing at something, but I couldn't keep my eyes open long enough to tell what. My consciousness was slipping.

I wished I could ask M6 for a diagnosis, but my helmet had been removed long ago. At some point, I closed my eyes—and that's when the vision began.

I wasn't a third-person observer this time.
I was there. Standing on a shoreline, staring out at a vast ocean. I could hear crashing waves, feel the cold breeze against my skin, even smell the salt in the air.

And beside me, someone held my hand.

Glancing over, I realized it was the pirate captain. She had a warm, congenial smile on her face. I felt...happy.

Until the sun turned bright white—then exploded.

The shockwave hit, and the vision shifted.

Now I was a bodiless observer flying through a massive space battle. Some of the ships were unmistakably human. Others were Artran warships. Still more belonged to species I didn't recognize. All of them were engaged in combat against a singular, wedge-shaped dreadnought.

It was enormous—spanning the size of several space stations. It fired devastating beams that sliced effortlessly through capital ships. No resistance. No chance.

Before I could gather my thoughts, I was thrust inside one of the larger alien warships battling the dreadnought. The crew were red-skinned, lizard-like beings clad in full armor. Many carried the same alien weapon I had found back on Zytec.

Just as I began moving through the ship, the vision shifted again.

Now I was rocketing past the battle, down toward a dark, barely visible planet.

Something about it called to me. I needed to see its surface. I needed to know what these aliens truly looked like.

But I never got the chance.

The planet swallowed me in darkness.

And the vision changed again.

I was back in first person. Hands gripping the railing of my apartment balcony. The sky was overcast. The city below bustled with life. People hurried through the streets.

I felt someone behind me and turned.

It was my wife.

She stood in the doorway, smiling softly. I embraced her. Held her close. Felt her warmth and the softness of her kiss.

"I've missed you so much," I whispered, letting the emotion flow freely.

She didn't respond with words. Instead, she stepped back and pointed skyward.

I turned to look. A bright white explosion bloomed in the sky.

I knew what it meant. I turned back to her—needing to see her face once more.

Her final words were:
"Seek the silent rift."

The vision vanished, swallowed by blackness.

What followed were flickering moments of lucidity. I remember being strapped into a chair.
I saw faces—dirty, unfamiliar. People I didn't recognize sat across from me, watching with wary eyes.

I didn't have the strength to ask questions. My body felt disjointed. Like my mind was one place, and the rest of me was somewhere else.

I tried to lift my left hand—it barely twitched. My right arm moved more easily, but it was weak.
My heart raced.

Something was *wrong* with me.

But I couldn't figure out what.

I blacked out again.

***

The next thing I remember was floating through a dim corridor bathed in red light. A demon looked down at me, and beside him walked the woman—the pirate captain. She was talking to someone, but I couldn't focus on who.

My eyes stayed locked on her.

She was beautiful. The memory of her holding my hand on that beach came flooding back, and for a moment, I felt peace. I felt happy.

Somehow, I willed my left hand to move—just enough to brush the fabric of her stained jumpsuit.

It took her a moment to realize what was happening. Then she reached down, took my hand in hers, and leaned closer.

The scent of strawberries—her shampoo—filled my senses.

I tried to squeeze her hand. Tried to pull her closer.
But my body wouldn't obey.

That's when it hit me.

This wasn't just exhaustion. This wasn't fatigue.
Something inside me had broken. A stroke, maybe. Or a brain aneurysm.

She looked down at me and spoke softly.

"Jack, you saved them all."

Saved who?

"We're going to take care of you," she said with a smile.

A sudden pinch in my right arm.

And everything faded to black again.

Chapter: Fifty-Nine

Several weeks had passed, and strangely enough, I found myself back on the planet with the beach from my vision. I had been walking along the shore for hours, trying to clear my thoughts and just be in the moment.

So much had happened since I was rescued from the Artran base.

Somehow, the team of Voidborn soldiers had managed to rescue all of the hostages the Artran had taken.

I was praised by everyone for that. Many had openly said the mission was a suicide run and that none of us would come back. But we did—with great success. In fact, only a few of the Voidborn soldiers had lost their lives during the raid.

Everyone hailed us as heroes.

However, every time I looked up at the night sky, a sense of dread filled me. It was as if an unseen force were watching—observing my every move.

I never felt alone anymore.

Even in the small cabin I inhabit, I always feel like someone is watching me. I haven't bothered trying to shake the feeling. Instead, I've made several attempts to telepathically counter whatever presence is observing me—but with no success.

The strokes I suffered under the intense telepathic battle with the obelisk alien left me weakened. I walk with a slight limp, and my left arm responds more slowly than it should. All of it is improving—just too slowly for my liking.

There's an urge inside me. A feeling that I *should* be doing something. That I need to learn more about Ethan and where he might have fled.

That inquiry could probably be answered by Sophia, but she managed to escape the Voidborn base with the Medusa, killing only two people in her wake. That feat alone increased her threat level in my mind. And now, I'm convinced she had everything to do with Ethan's escape.

As I neared the path to my cabin, I sat down in the sand and watched the sun begin its descent over the horizon. It was going to be a beautiful sunset—beams of red and orange painted the clouds above. Far off in the distance, a purple haze hinted at a storm lurking just beyond the horizon.

Nearby, I heard the flomp of someone approaching in sandals, just barely audible over the crashing waves. I didn't need to look. I already knew who it was.

Captain Kayla Riven of the Voidborn pirates sat down beside me in the sand. For the past couple of weeks, she'd been checking in—seeing how my recovery was going. We both had a fondness for the local seafood dishes the nearby chef served.

She didn't say anything at first—just gave me a quick glance, then turned her gaze to the setting sun.

I found comfort in her companionship. And despite both of our reluctance to admit it, I felt like a bond was forming between us. For the first time in a long while… I felt happy.

As the sky darkened and the last embers of sunlight faded away, we looked at each other—and that's when the vision struck.

I saw three soldiers in Ghost Recon armor surrounding us, weapons raised, ready to strike.
I could feel their tension. They had orders to kill.

I considered lashing out with my abilities—but something about the lead soldier felt familiar.
Their thoughts radiated toward me—conflicted, uncertain. Understandable.

Raising my arms slowly, which caused Kayla to grab at me in confusion, I spoke clearly.

"Beverly, please don't kill us," I said. "Despite the face you see—I *am* Jack Donovan. Your mother's maiden name is Charlotte."

I stood now, Kayla beside me, still gripping my arm and whispering questions I didn't hear.

All of my focus was locked on the figure before me.

The lead Ghost Recon soldier unphased and stepped forward. Then, after a pause, they removed their helmet—and I found myself looking at the young, beautiful face of Beverly.

"Jack?" she said, squinting at me. "How is this possible?"

"We have a lot to talk about," I said.

She lowered her rifle and stepped closer—and to my surprise, we embraced.

She pulled me into a hug, whispering into my ear:
"I should've stayed closer to you. I should've had your back on Mars."

"Everything's fine," I replied softly.
"Nothing else matters more than this moment."

www.ingramcontent.com/pod-product-compliance
Lightning Source LLC
Chambersburg PA
CBHW070525310726

48976CB00002BA/544